D0394409

# Dear Parent:

## *Psst . . . you're looking at the Super Secret Weapon of Reading. It's called comics.*

**STEP INTO READING® COMIC READERS** are a perfect step in learning to read. They provide visual cues to the meaning of words and helpfully break out short pieces of dialogue into speech balloons.

Here are some terms commonly associated with comics:

PANEL: A section of a comic with a box drawn around it.
CAPTION: Narration that helps set the scene.
SPEECH BALLOON: A bubble containing dialogue.
GUTTER: The space between panels.

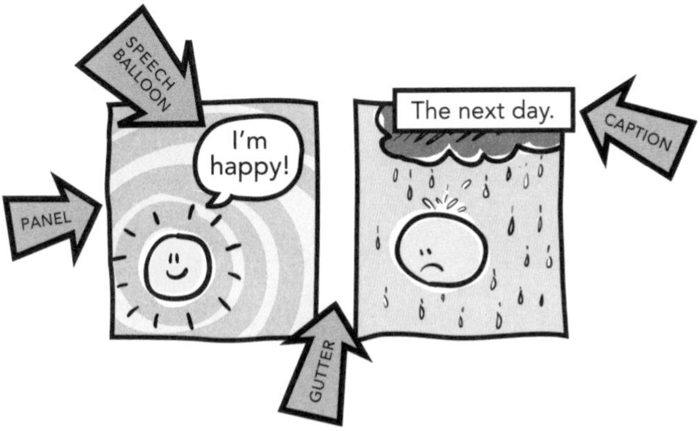
SPEECH BALLOON
I'm happy!
PANEL
The next day.
CAPTION
GUTTER

### *Tips for reading comics with your child:*

- **Have your child read the speech balloons while you read the captions.**
- **Ask your child: What is a character feeling? How can you tell?**
- **Have your child draw a comic showing what happens after the book is finished.**

**STEP INTO READING® COMIC READERS** are designed to engage and to provide an empowering reading experience. They are also fun. The best-kept secret of comics is that they create lifelong readers. *And that will make you the real hero of the story!*

Jennifer L. Holm and Matthew Holm
Co-creators of the Babymouse and Squish series

# To Caroline and Ben

Photograph credits: Cover: © Monica and Michael Sweet/Getty; pp. 4, 46, 48: © Medioimages/Photodisc/Getty; pp. 8, 19: © iStockphoto.com/DNY59; pp. 8–10, 26: © iStockphoto.com/joeygil; p. 9: © iStockphoto.com/Bike_Maverick; p. 10: © iStockphoto.com/SPrada; pp. 10–13, 48: © iStockphoto.com/tiler84; p. 14: © iStockphoto.com/slobo; pp. 16, 39, 40, 47: © iStockphoto.com/Mlenny; pp. 19, 39: © Purestock/Getty; pp. 20–21: © iStockphoto.com/RonTech2000; p. 21: © iStockphoto.com/tbd; p. 21: © iStockphoto.com/Frantysek; p. 21: © iStockphoto.com/Maliketh; p. 21: © iStockphoto.com/sorendls; p. 22: © iStockphoto.com/beklaus; p. 23: © iStockphoto.com/ejs9; p. 24: © iStockphoto.com/TiannaChantal; p. 29: © iStockphoto.com/JackJelly; pp. 34, 37: © Kanaka Menehune/Getty; pp. 37, 48: © iStockphoto.com/rodho; p. 41: © iStockphoto.com/neosummer; pp. 43–44: © iStockphoto.com/Photomorphic.

Visit us on the Web!
StepIntoReading.com
randomhouse.com/kids

Educators and librarians, for a variety of teaching tools, visit us at RHTeachersLibrarians.com

*Library of Congress Cataloging-in-Publication Data*
Kredensor, Diane.
Ollie & Moon : aloha! / Diane Kredensor.
   p. cm.
Summary: "The newest adventure of two cat best friends is set on the exotic sandy beaches of Hawaii. When Ollie dares Moon to try something new, she learns about confronting her fears with the help of a friend."—Provided by publisher.
ISBN 978-0-307-97950-6 (trade) — ISBN 978-0-375-97131-0 (lib. bdg.) — ISBN 978-0-375-98129-6 (ebook) — ISBN 978-0-449-81426-0 (ebook with audio)
[1. Fear—Fiction. 2. Best friends—Fiction. 3. Friendship—Fiction. 4. Games—Fiction. 5. Hawaii—Fiction. 6. Cats—Fiction.] I. Title. II. Title: Ollie and Moon. III. Title: Aloha.
PZ7.K877Om 2013 [E]—dc23 2012019152

Printed in the United States of America
10 9 8 7 6 5 4 3 2 1

ING® STEP **3**

# OLLIE & MOON
# ALOHA!

A COMIC READER

by Diane Kredensor

Random House 🏠 New York

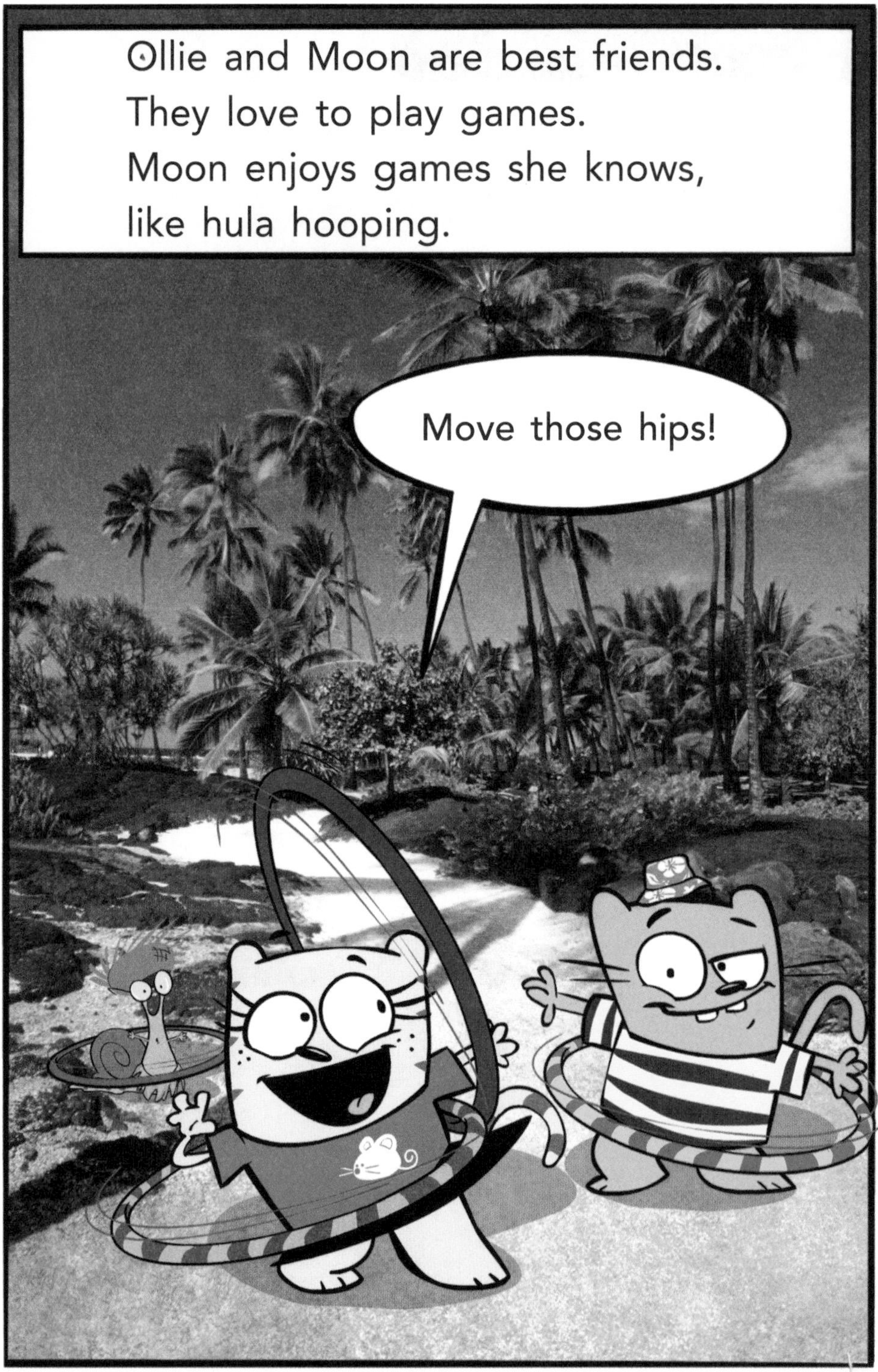
Ollie and Moon are best friends.
They love to play games.
Moon enjoys games she knows,
like hula hooping.
Move those hips!

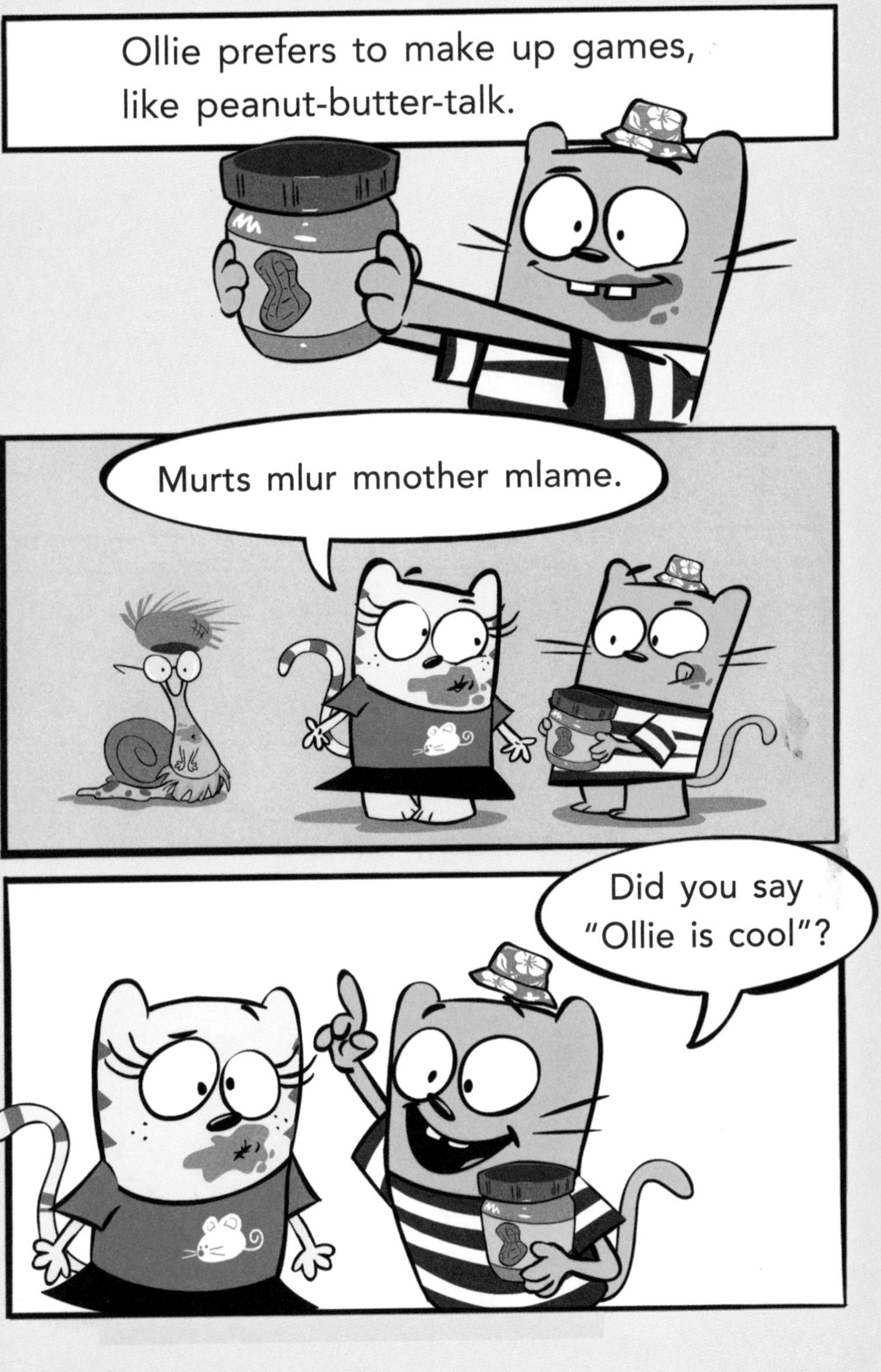
Ollie prefers to make up games, like peanut-butter-talk.
Murts mlur mnother mlame.
Did you say "Ollie is cool"?

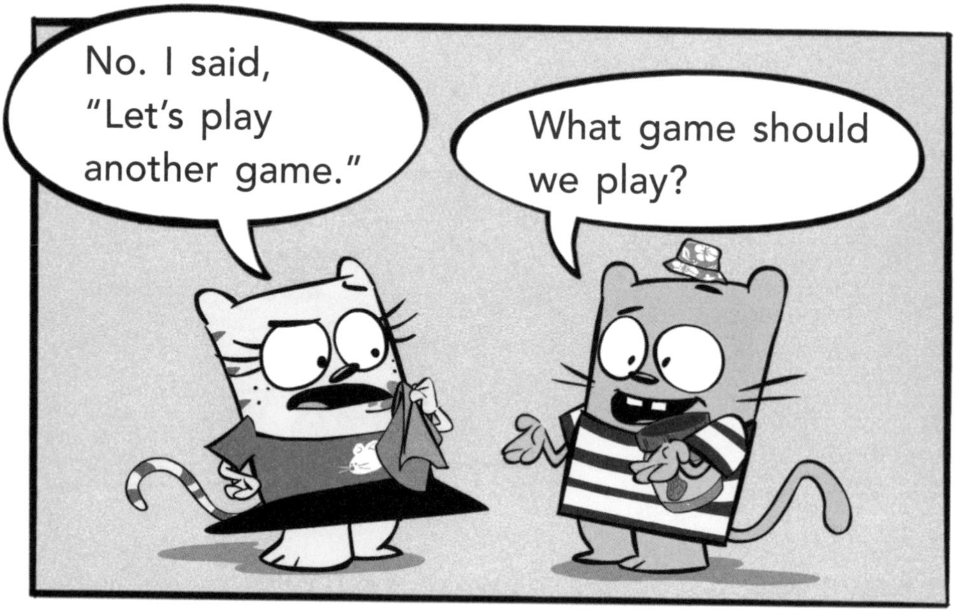
No. I said, "Let's play another game."
What game should we play?

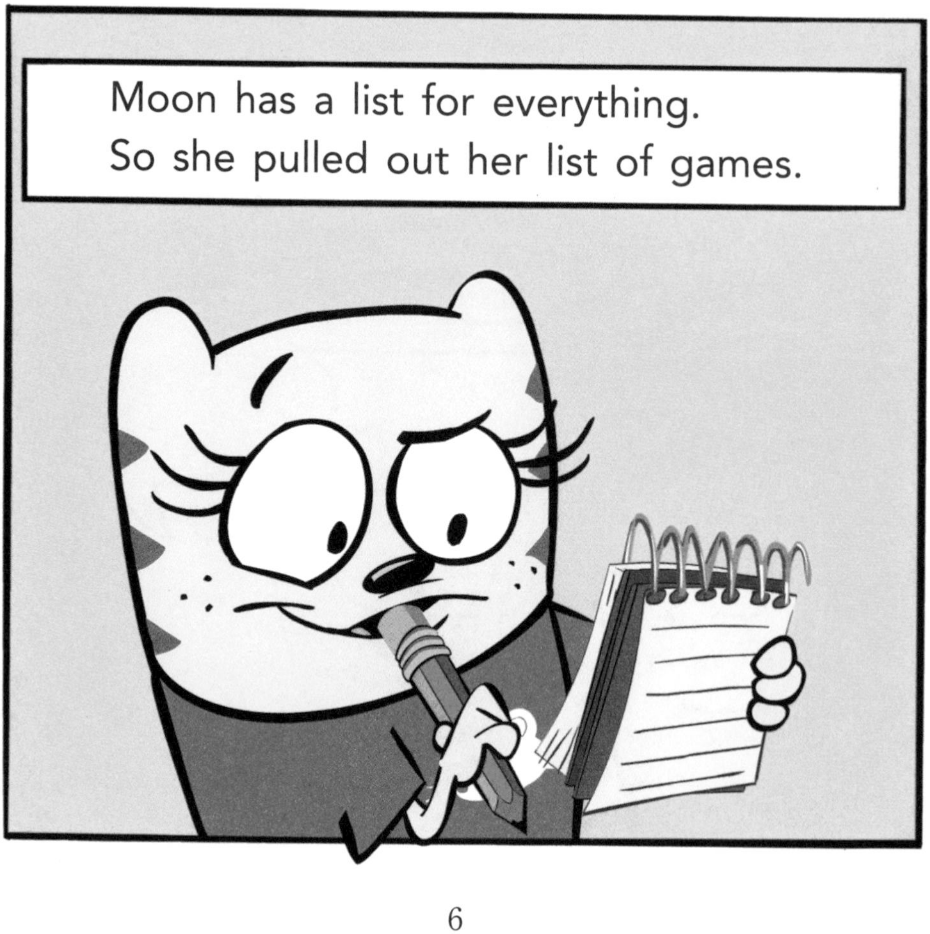
Moon has a list for everything.
So she pulled out her list of games.

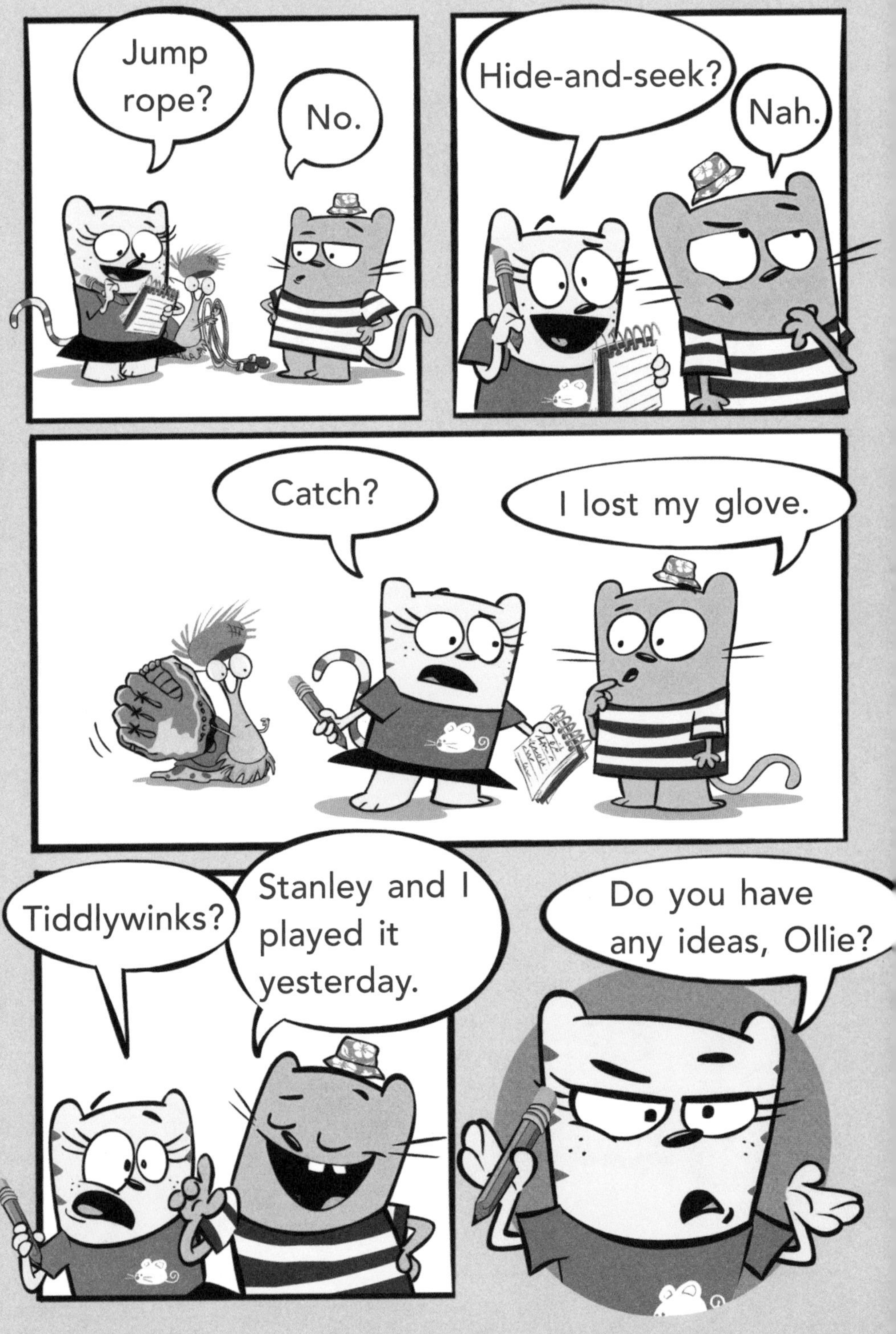
Jump rope?
No.
Hide-and-seek?
Nah.
Catch?
I lost my glove.
Tiddlywinks?
Stanley and I played it yesterday.
Do you have any ideas, Ollie?

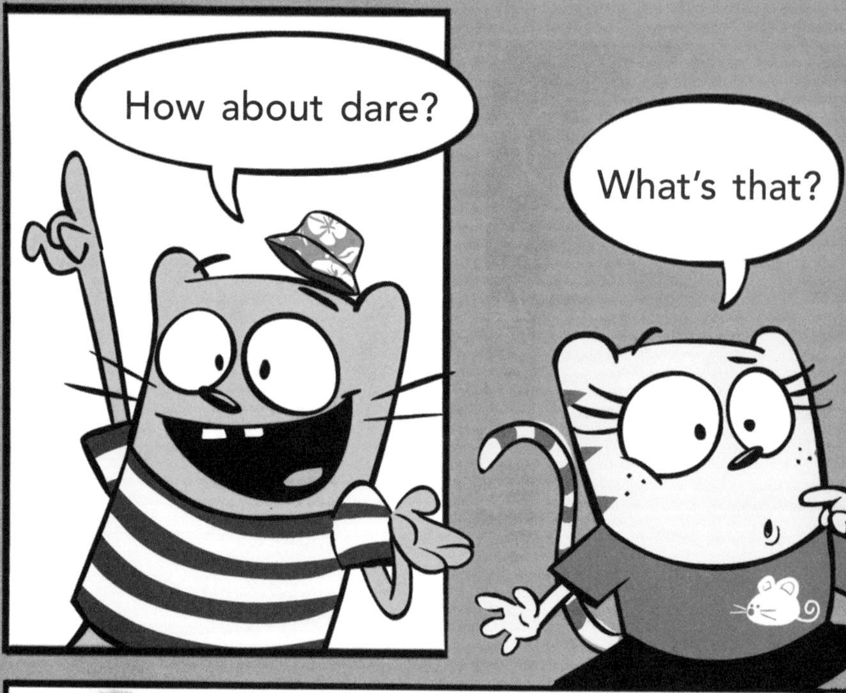
How about dare?
What's that?

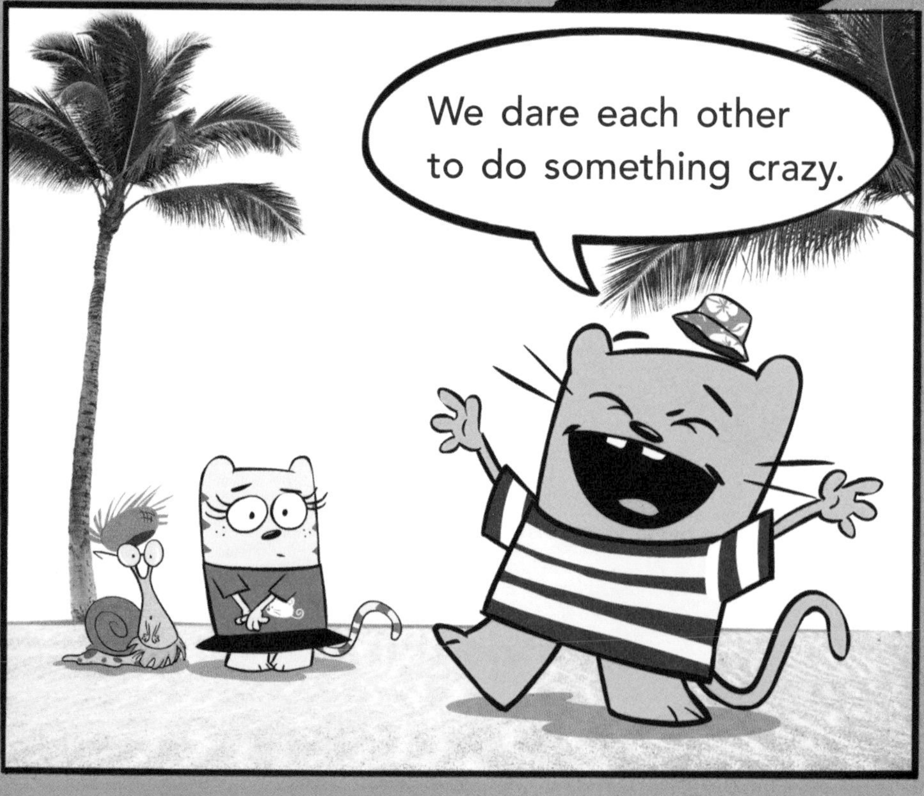
We dare each other
to do something crazy.

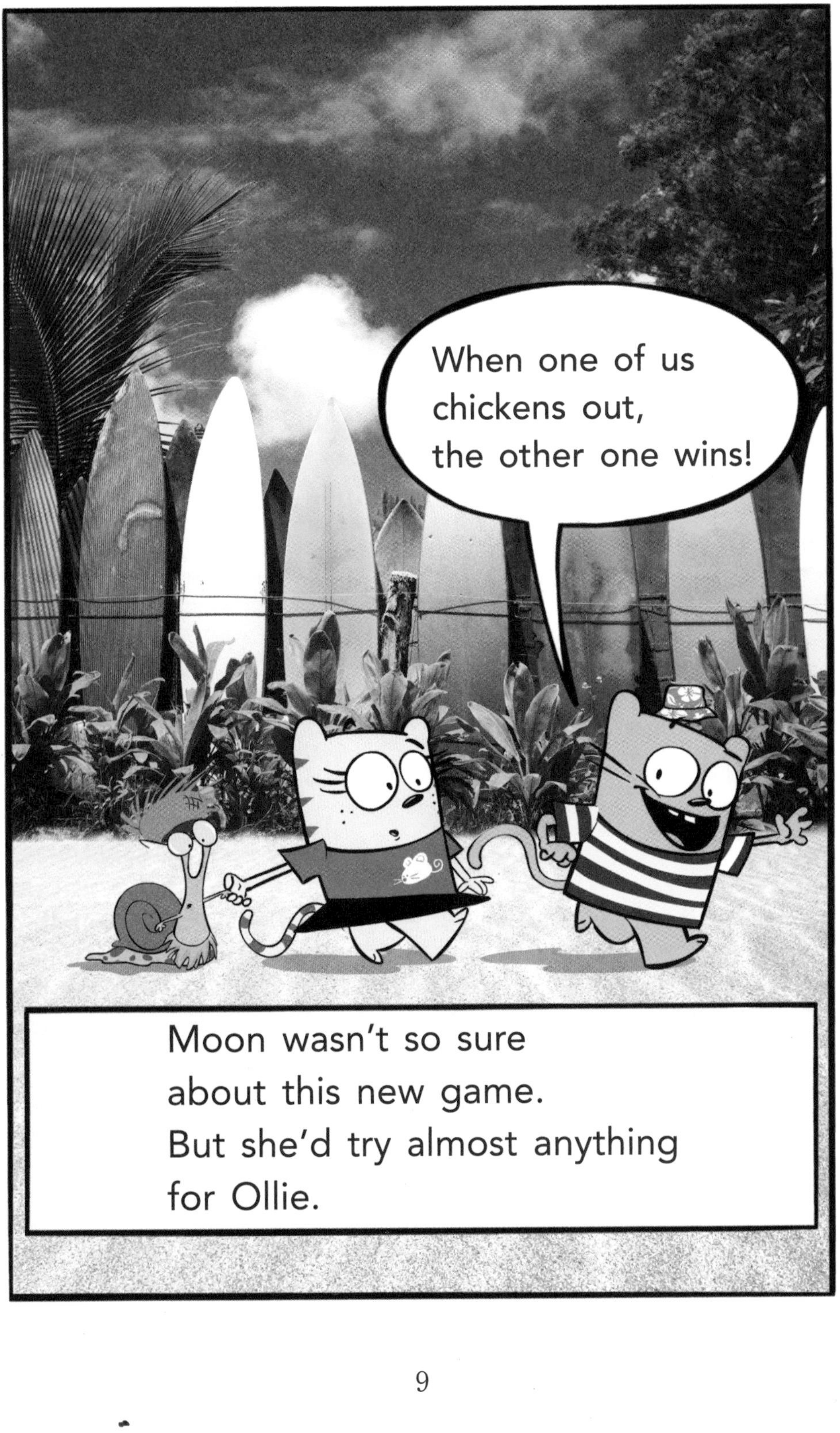
When one of us chickens out, the other one wins!

Moon wasn't so sure
about this new game.
But she'd try almost anything
for Ollie.

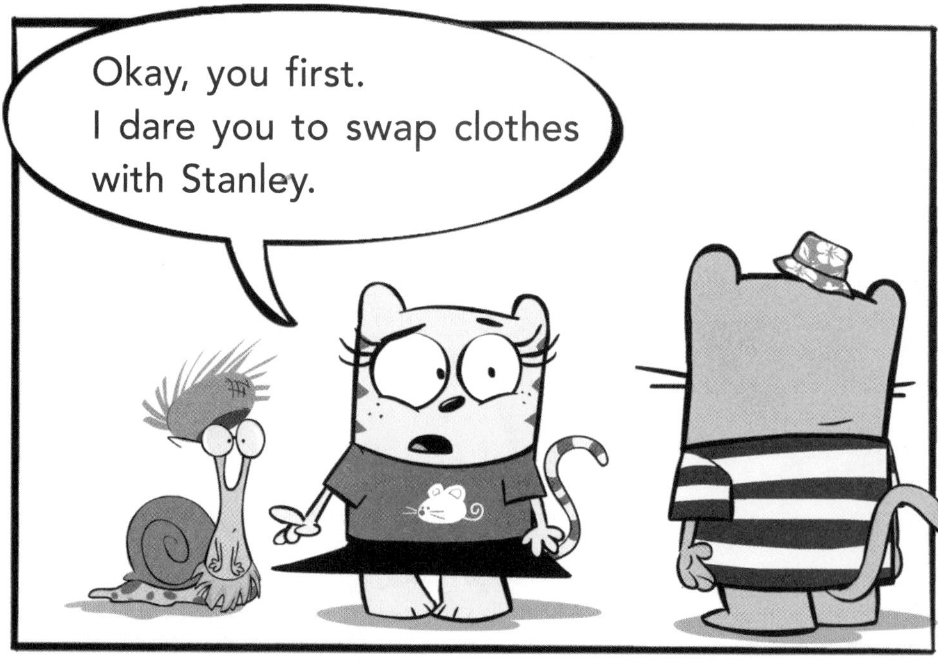
Okay, you first.
I dare you to swap clothes with Stanley.

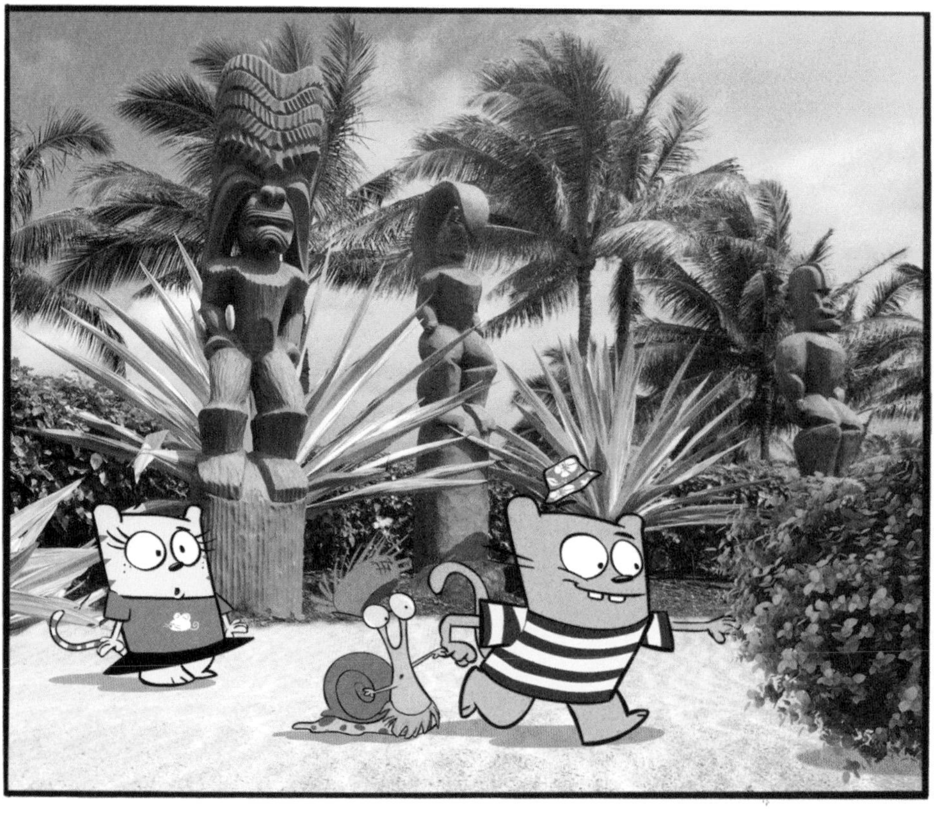

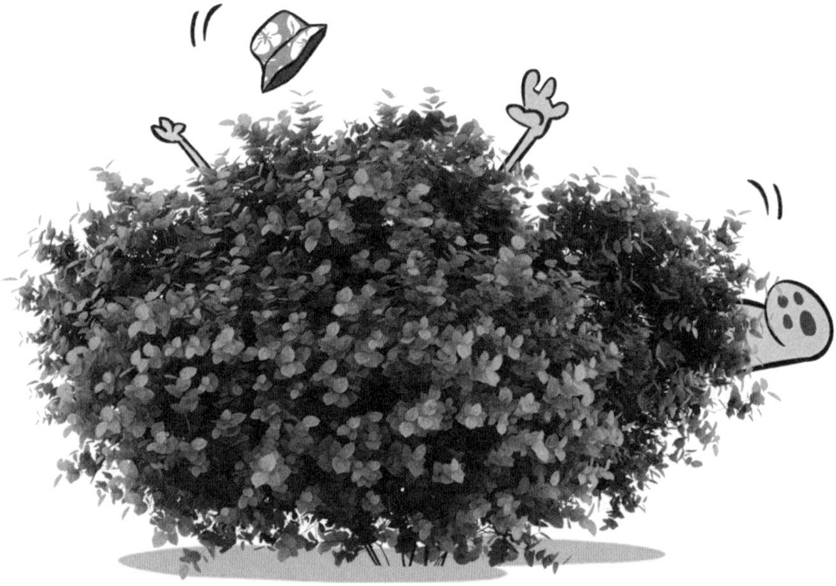

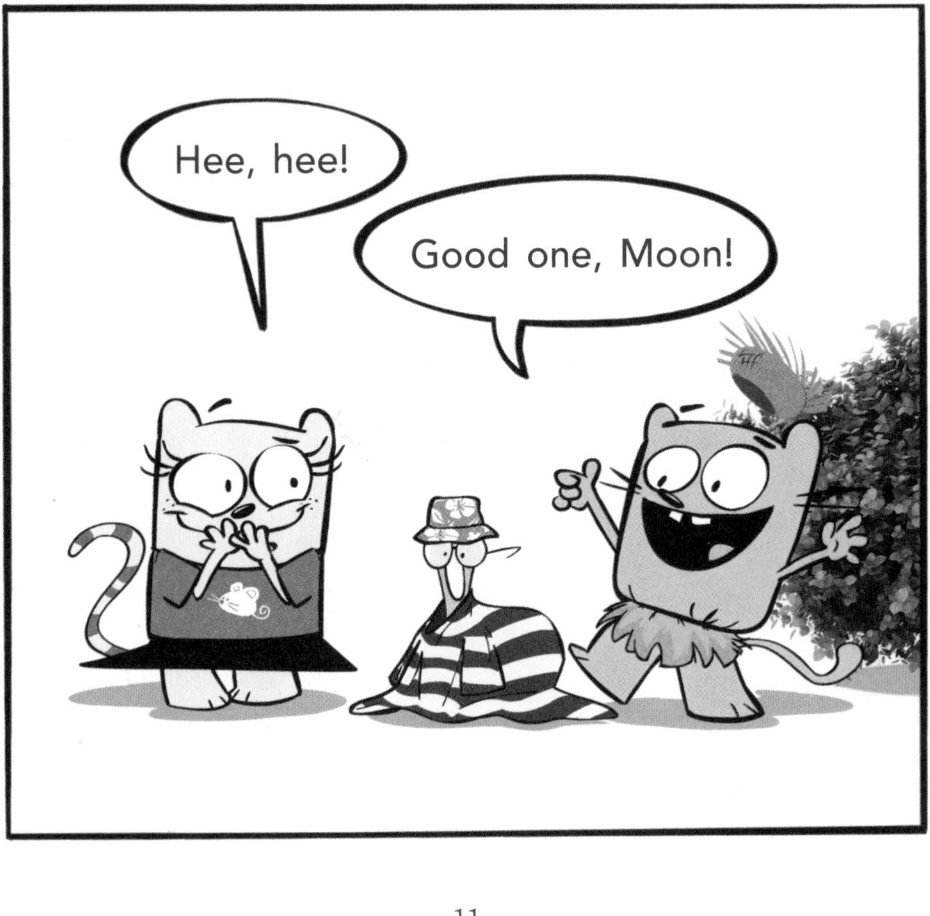
Hee, hee!
Good one, Moon!

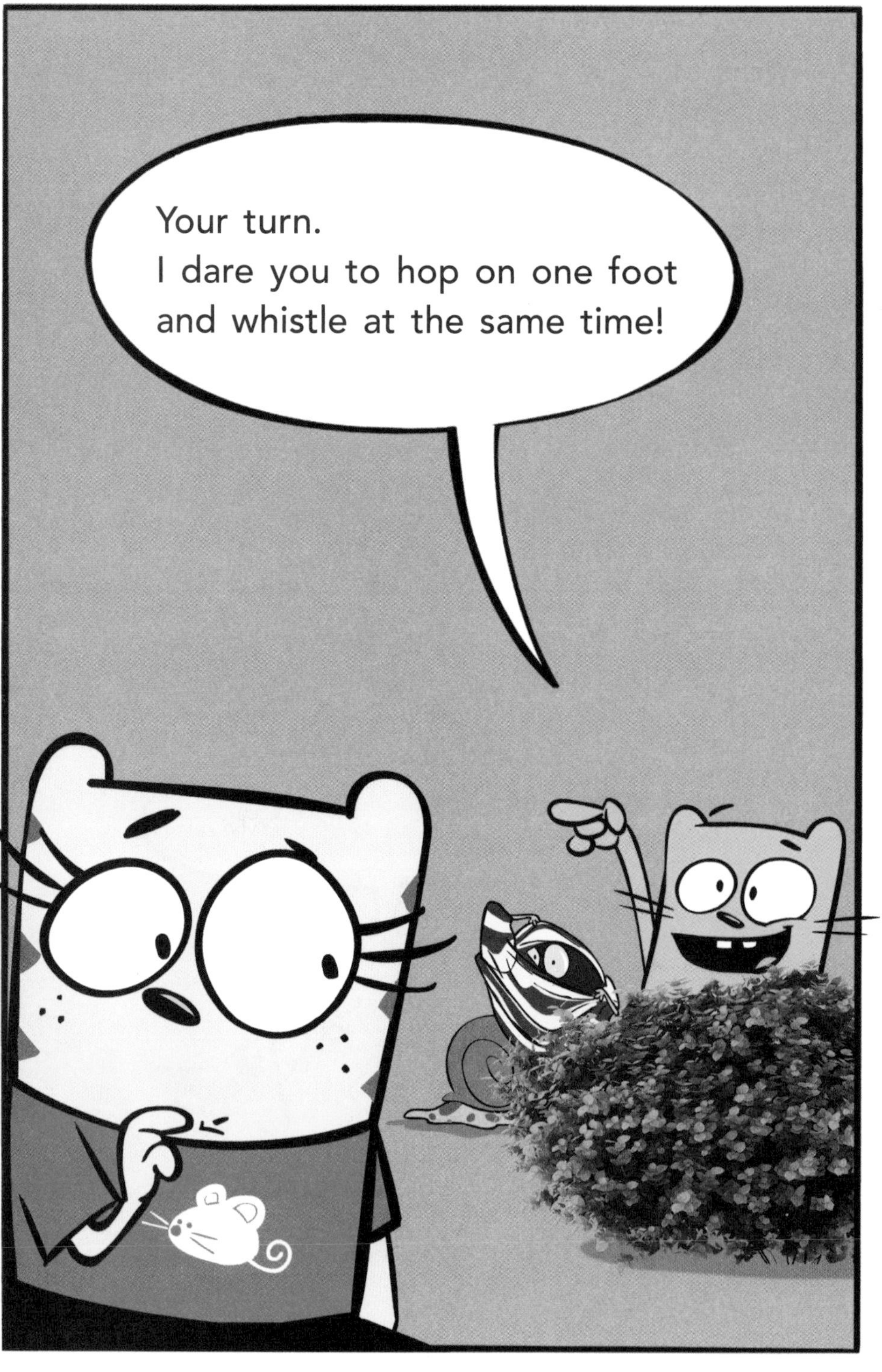
Your turn.
I dare you to hop on one foot
and whistle at the same time!

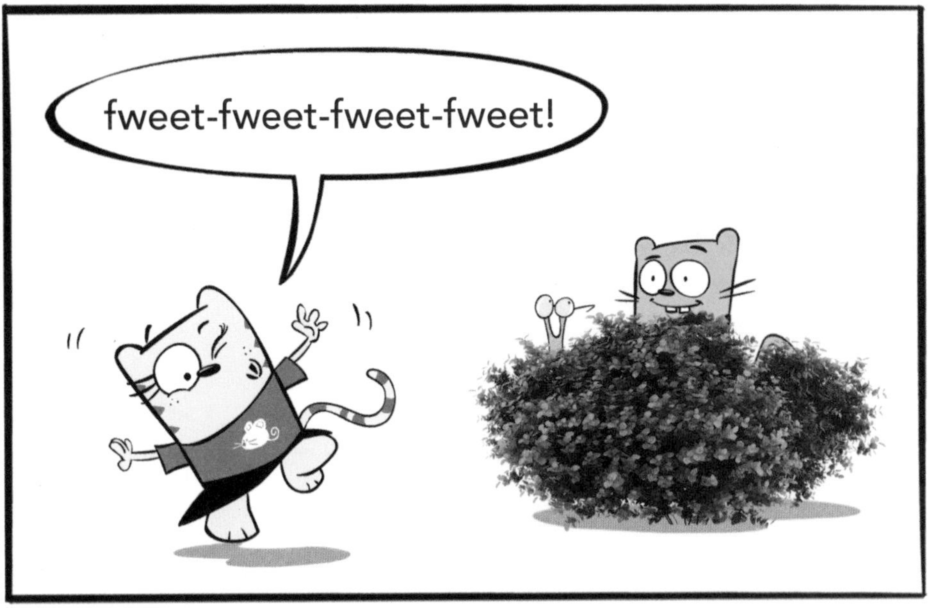
fweet-fweet-fweet-fweet!

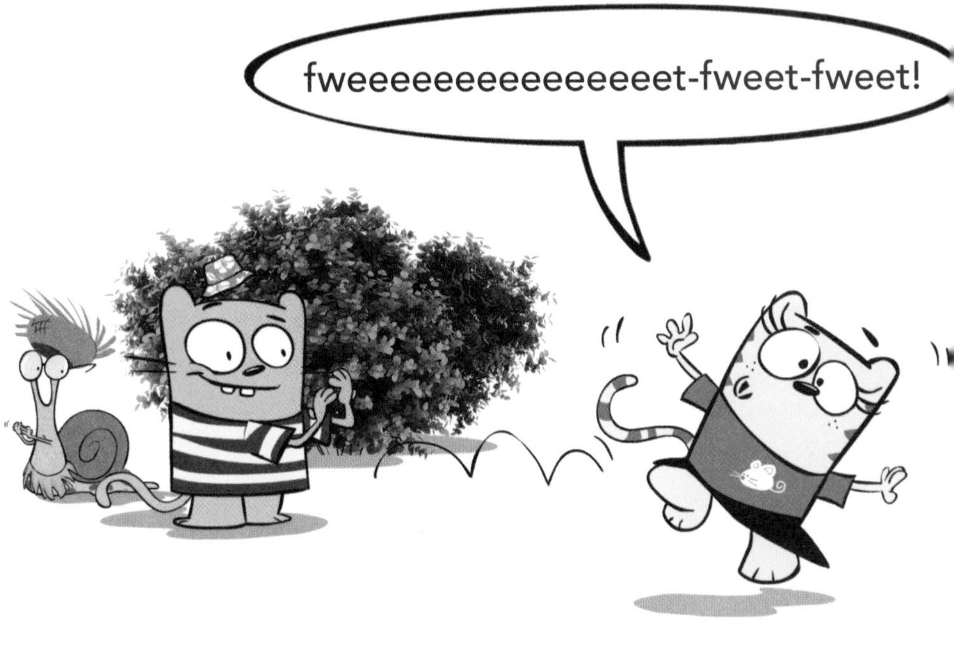
fweeeeeeeeeeeeeeet-fweet-fweet!

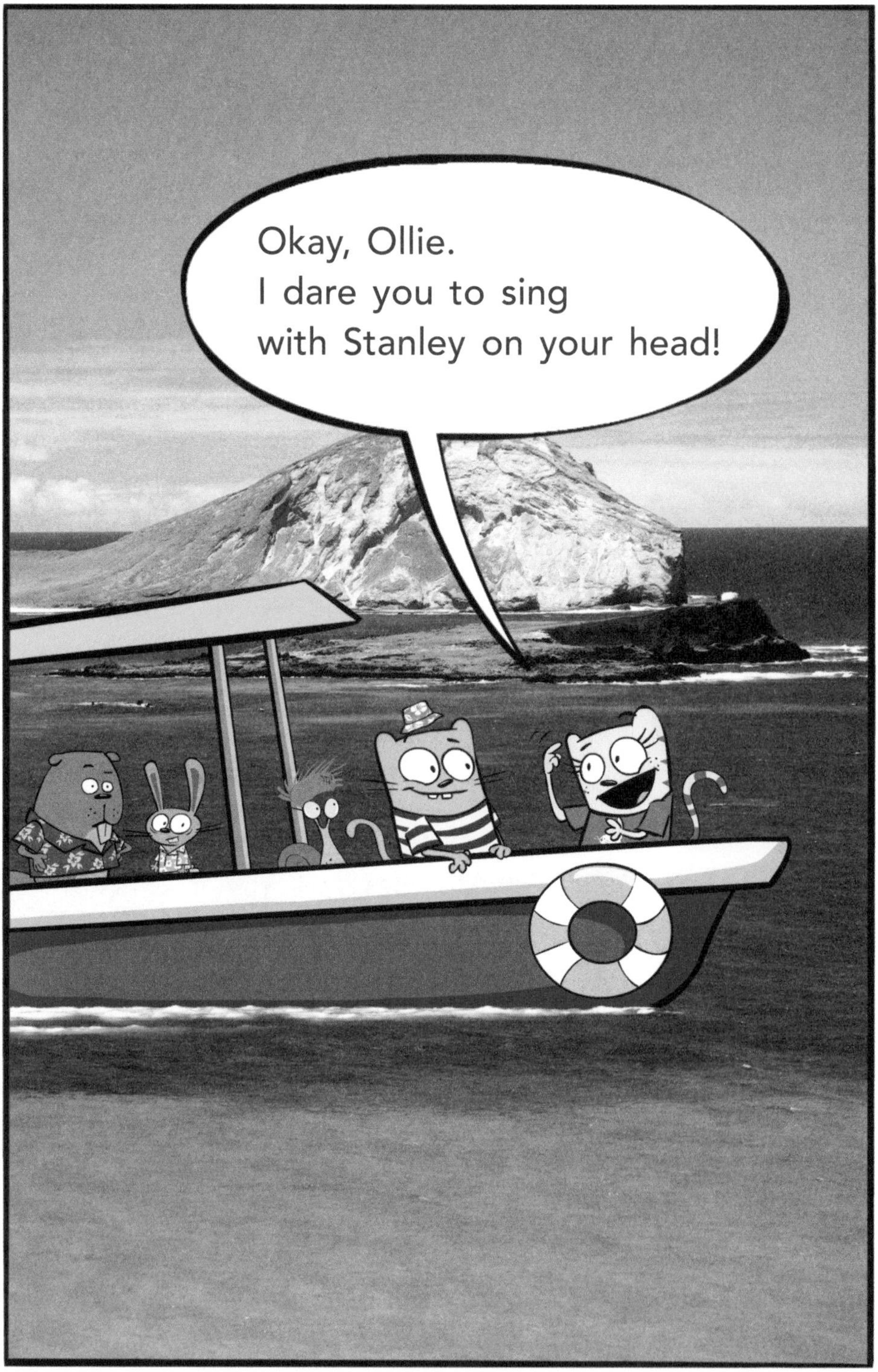
Okay, Ollie.
I dare you to sing
with Stanley on your head!

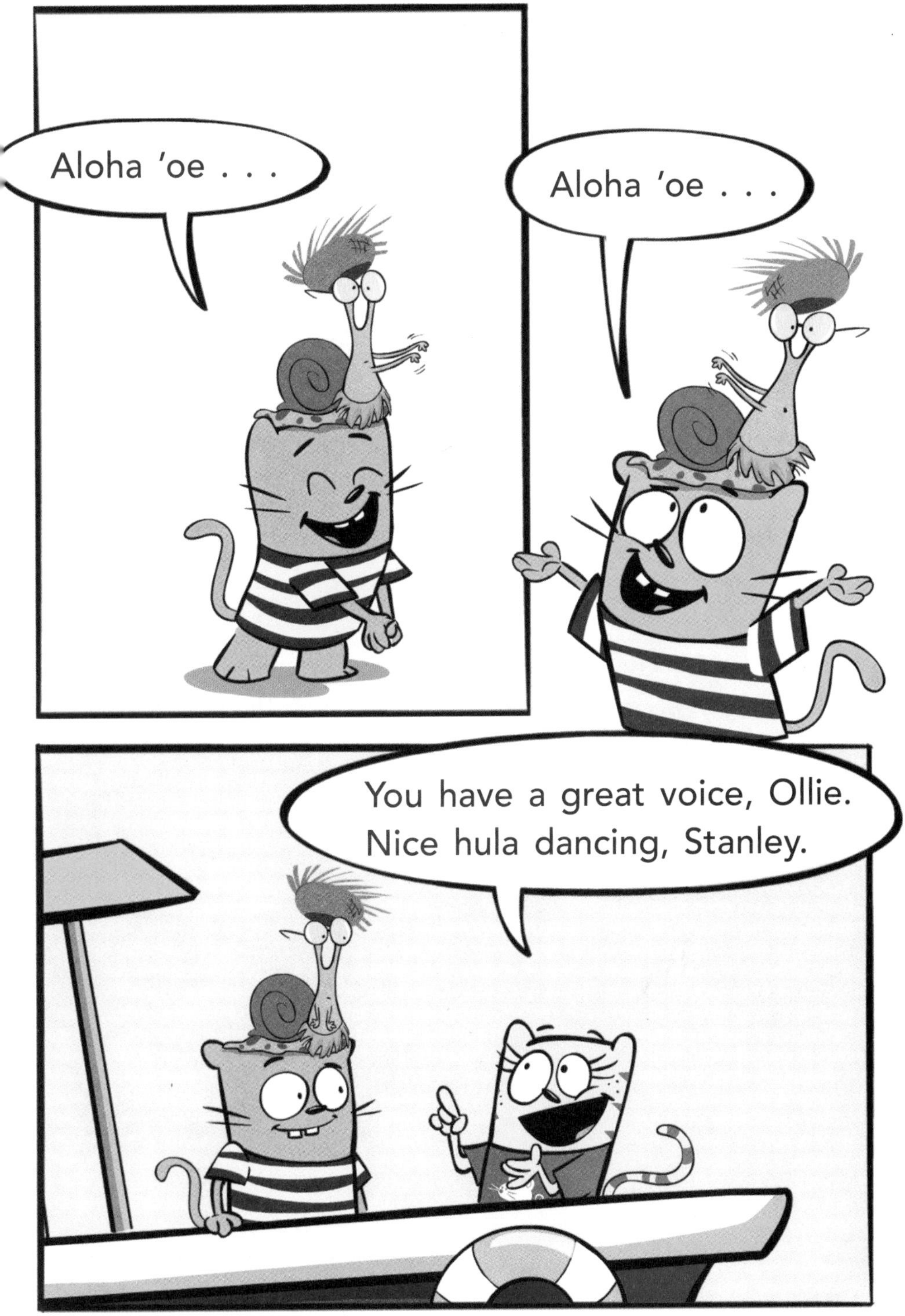
Aloha 'oe . . .
Aloha 'oe . . .
You have a great voice, Ollie. Nice hula dancing, Stanley.

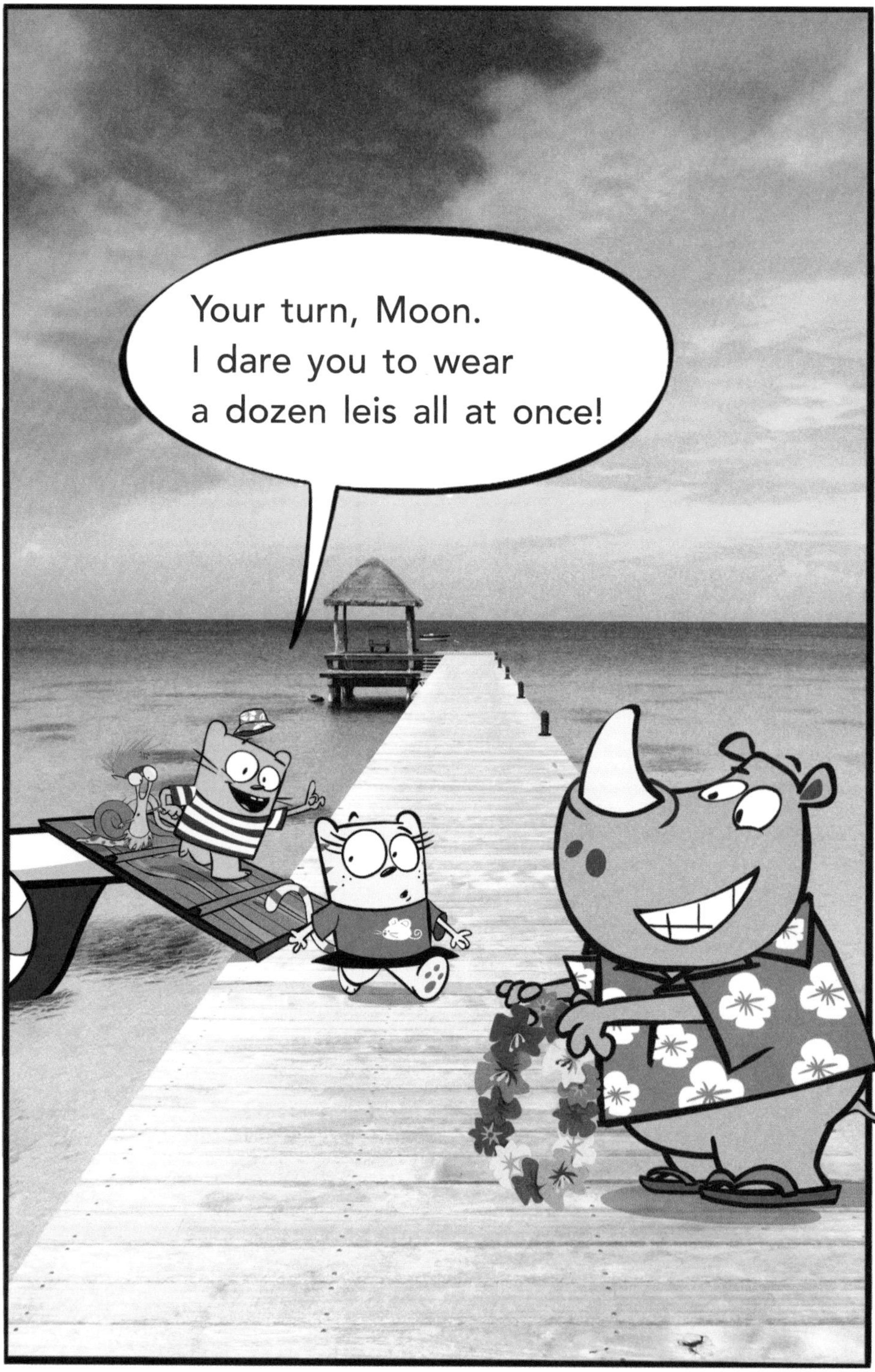
Your turn, Moon.
I dare you to wear
a dozen leis all at once!

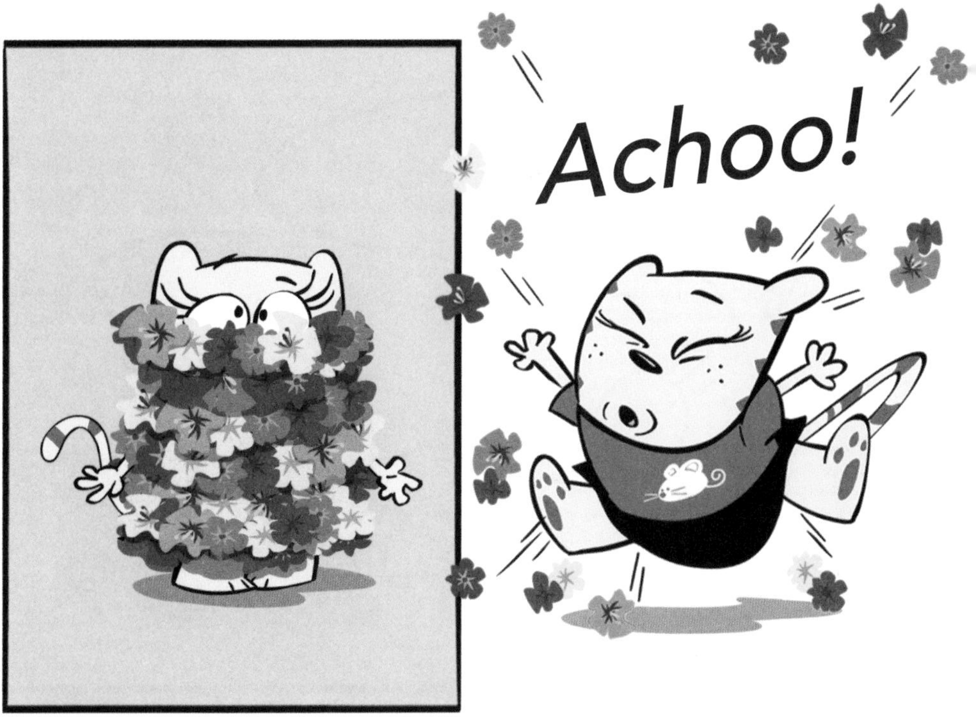
Achoo!

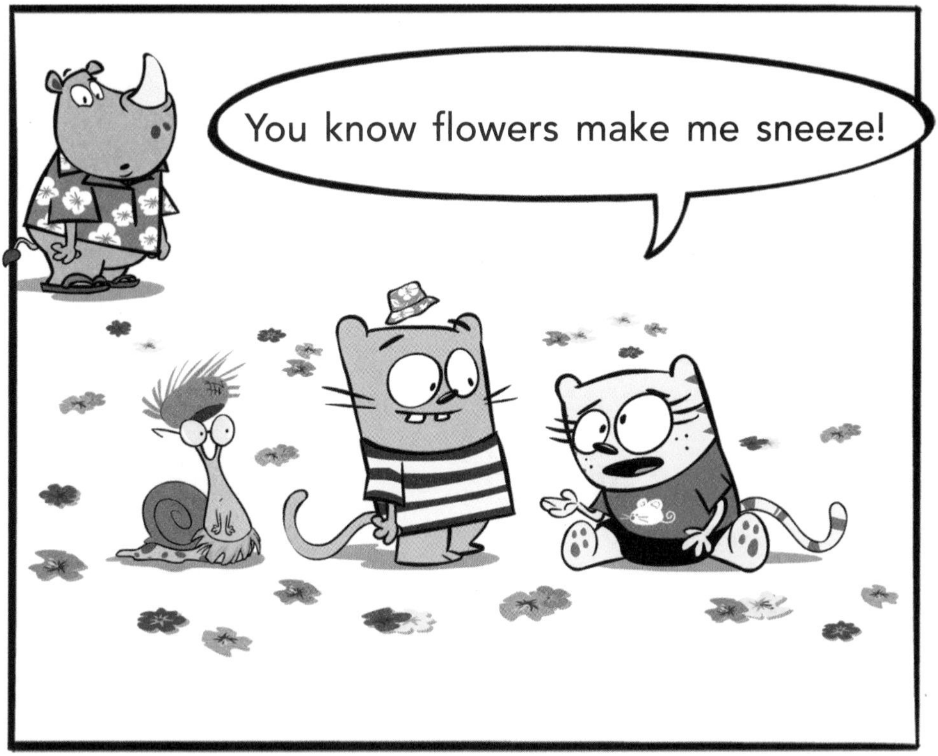
You know flowers make me sneeze!

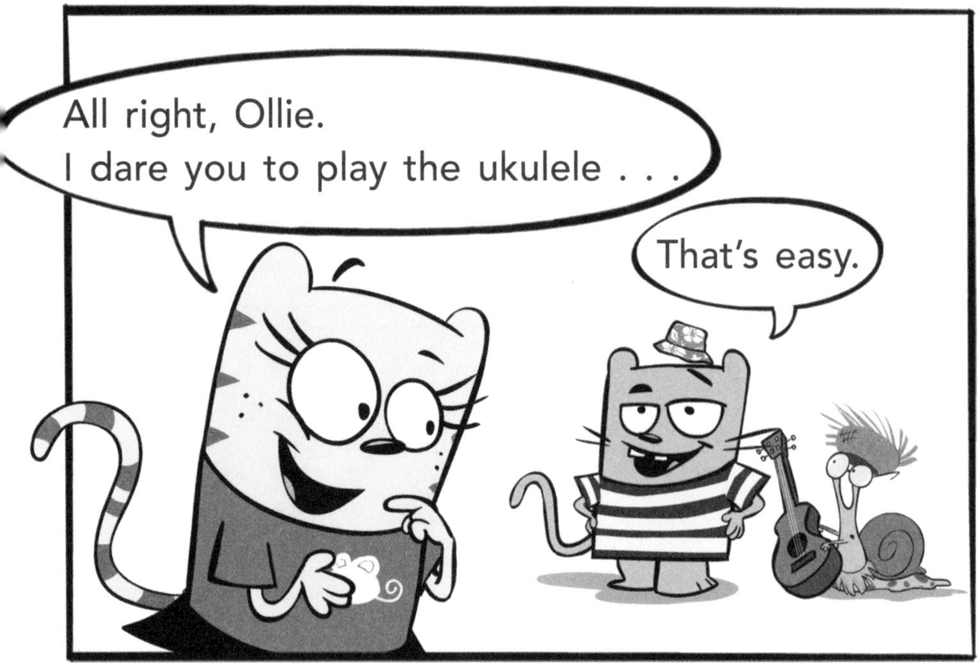
All right, Ollie.
I dare you to play the ukulele . . .
That's easy.

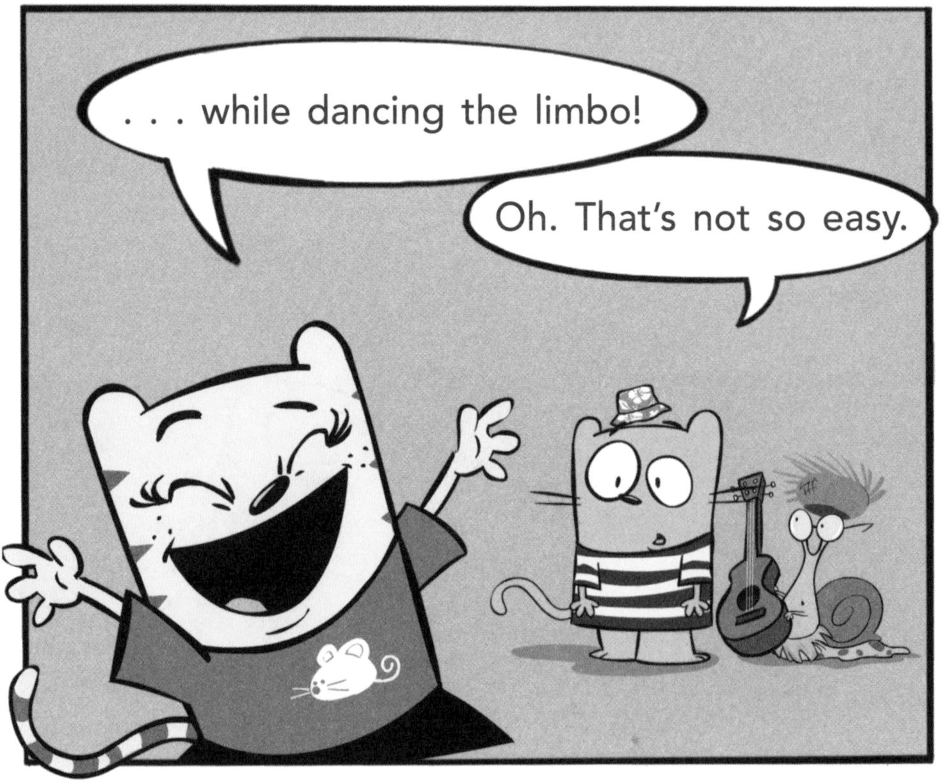
. . . while dancing the limbo!
Oh. That's not so easy.

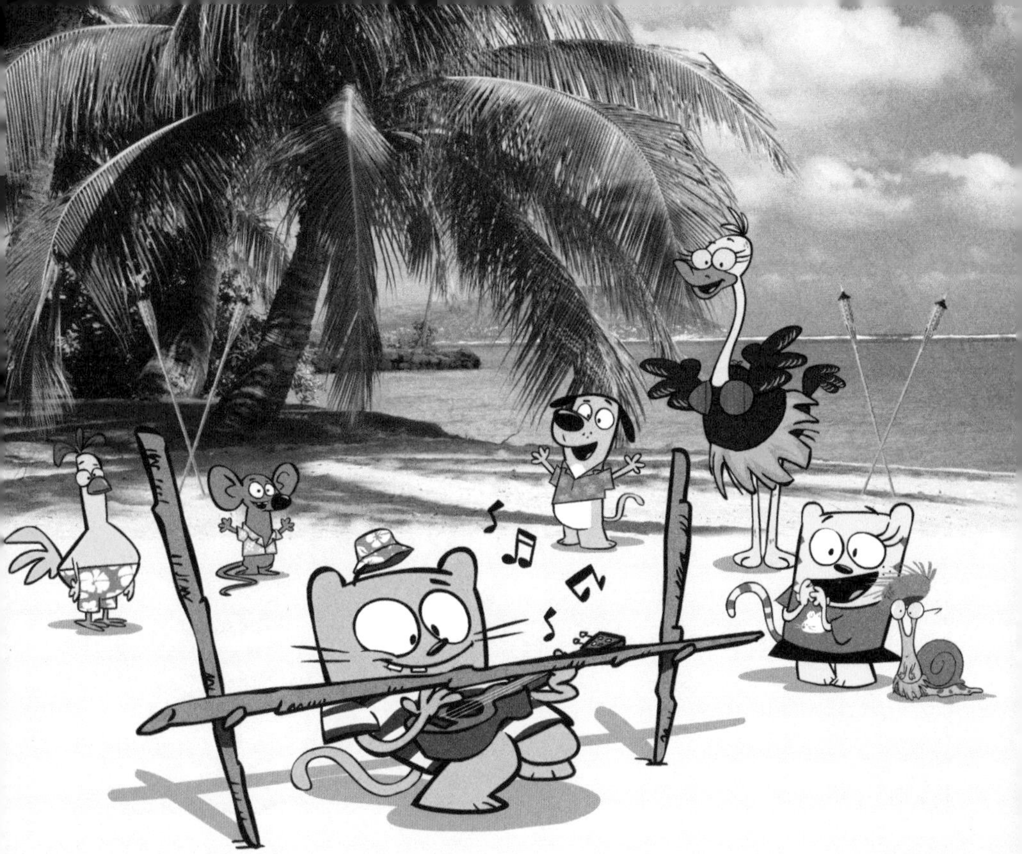

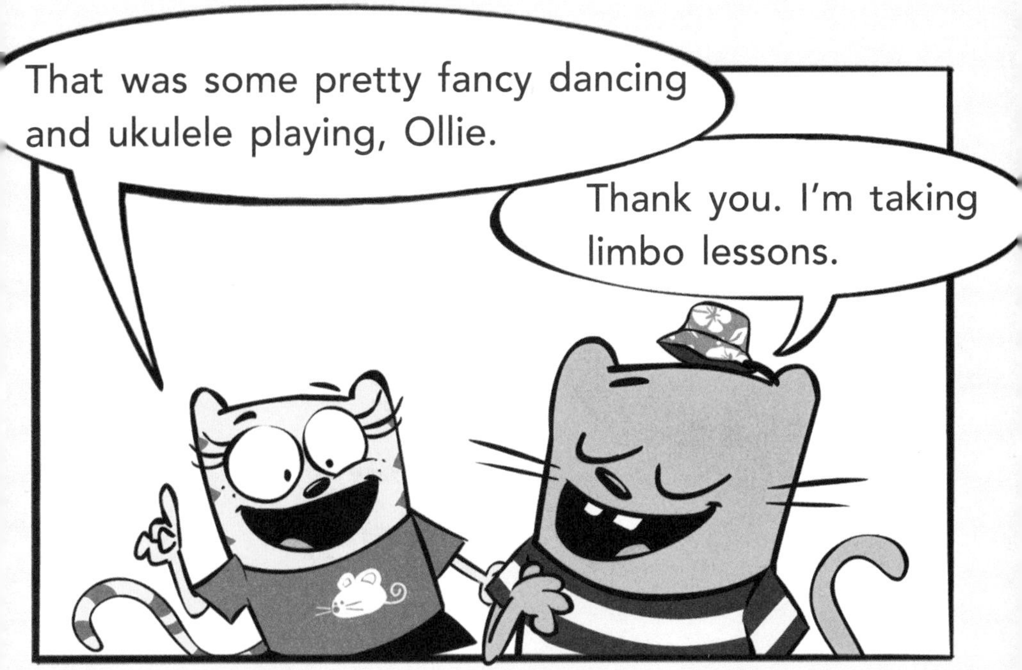
That was some pretty fancy dancing and ukulele playing, Ollie.
Thank you. I'm taking limbo lessons.

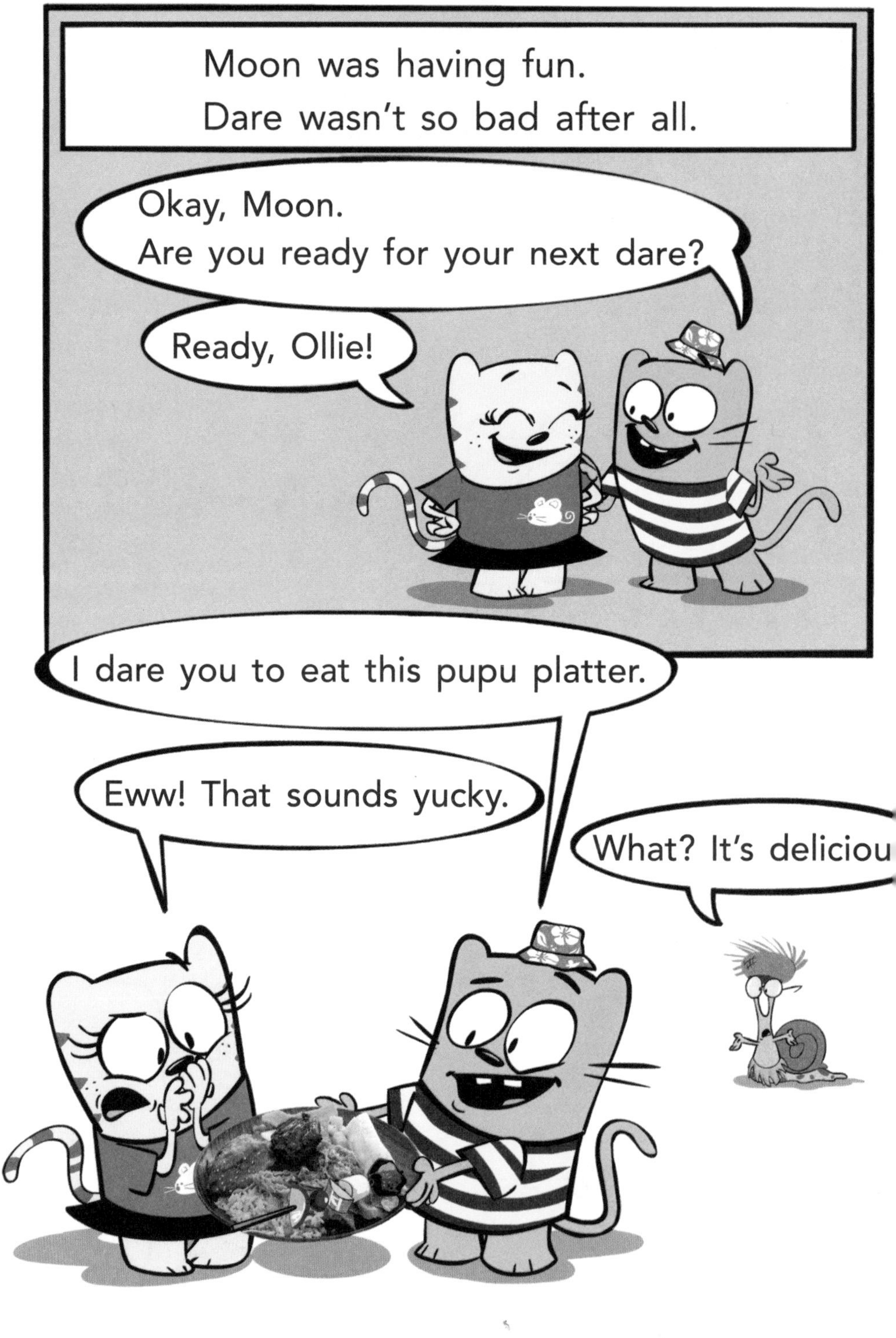
Moon was having fun.
Dare wasn't so bad after all.
Okay, Moon.
Are you ready for your next dare?
Ready, Ollie!
I dare you to eat this pupu platter.
Eww! That sounds yucky.
What? It's deliciou

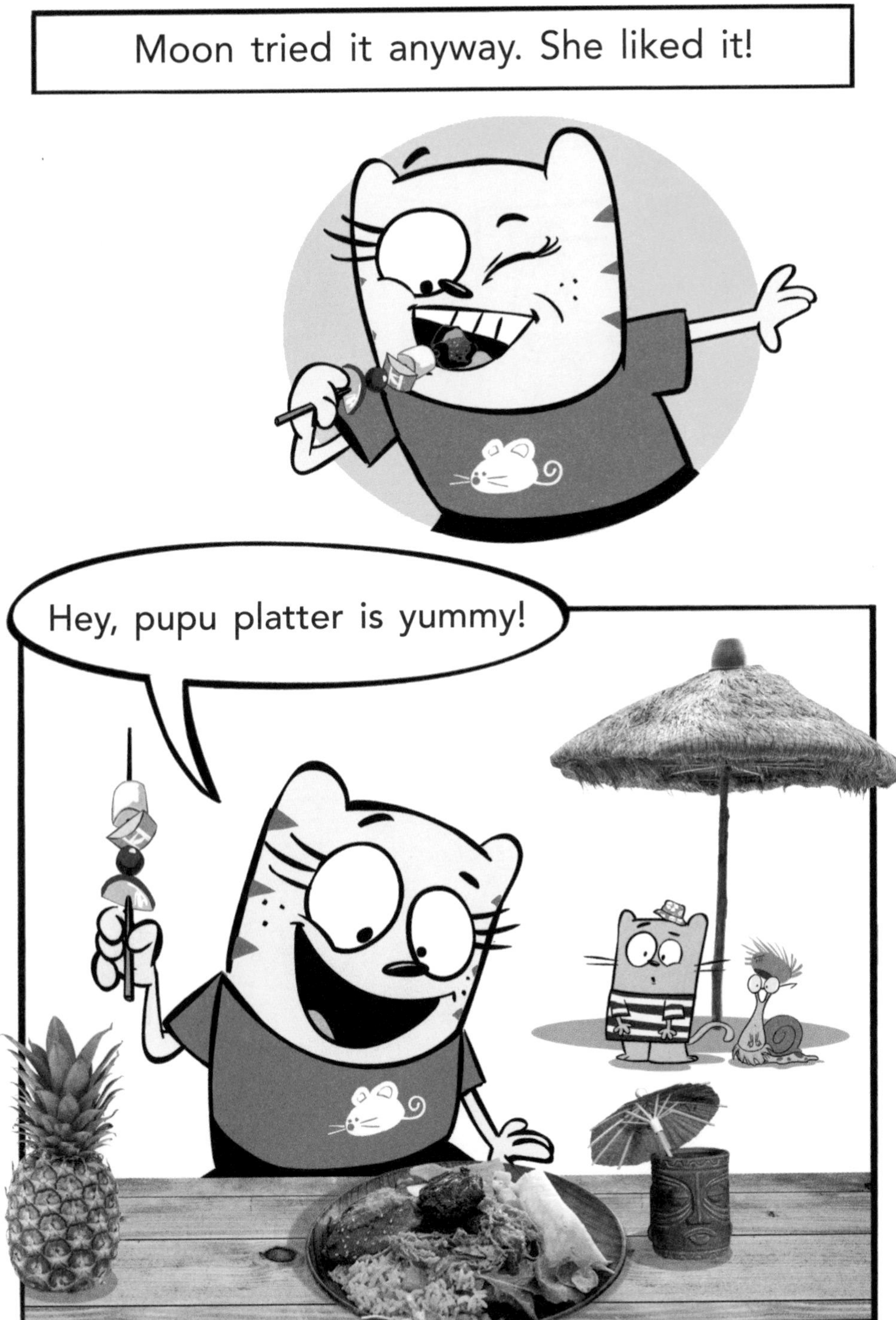
Moon tried it anyway. She liked it!
Hey, pupu platter is yummy!

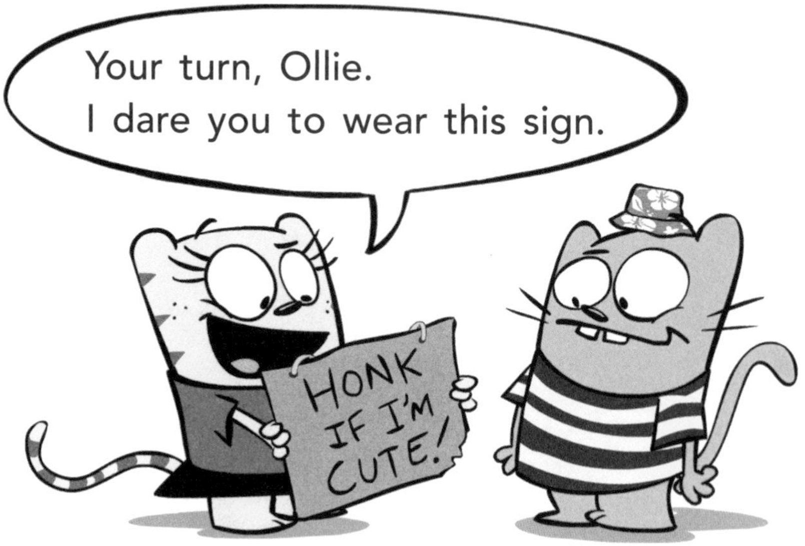
Your turn, Ollie.
I dare you to wear this sign.
HONK IF I'M CUTE!

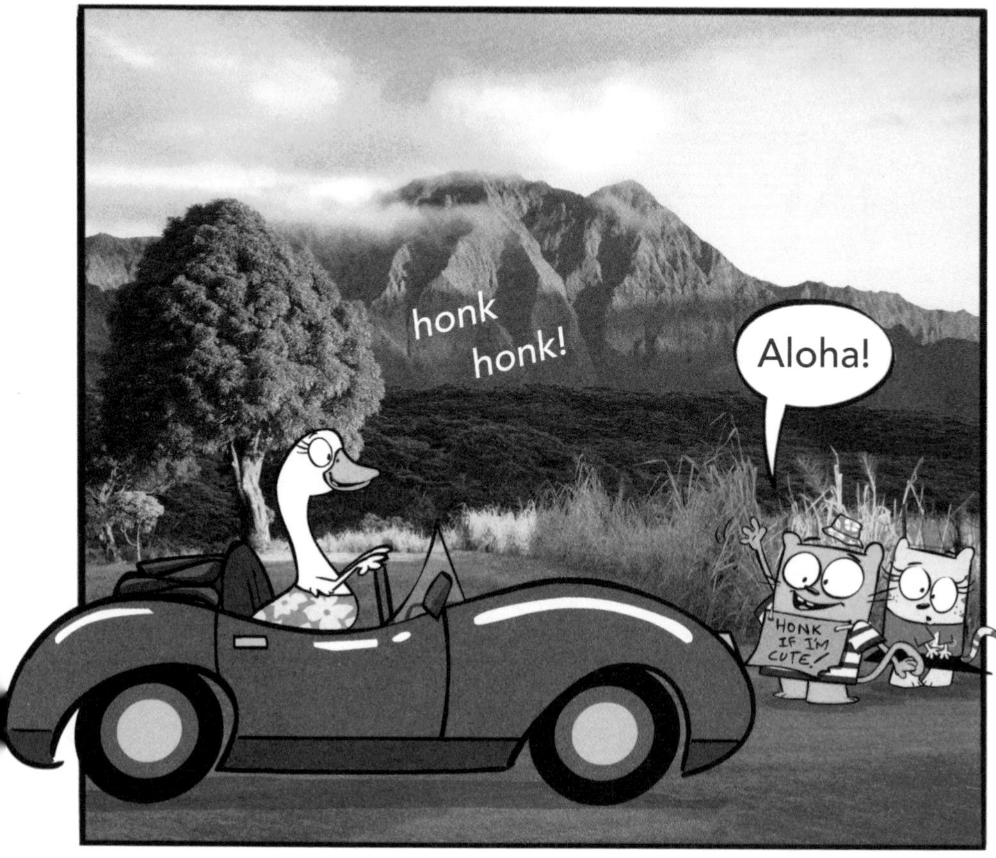
honk
honk!
Aloha!
HONK IF I'M CUTE!

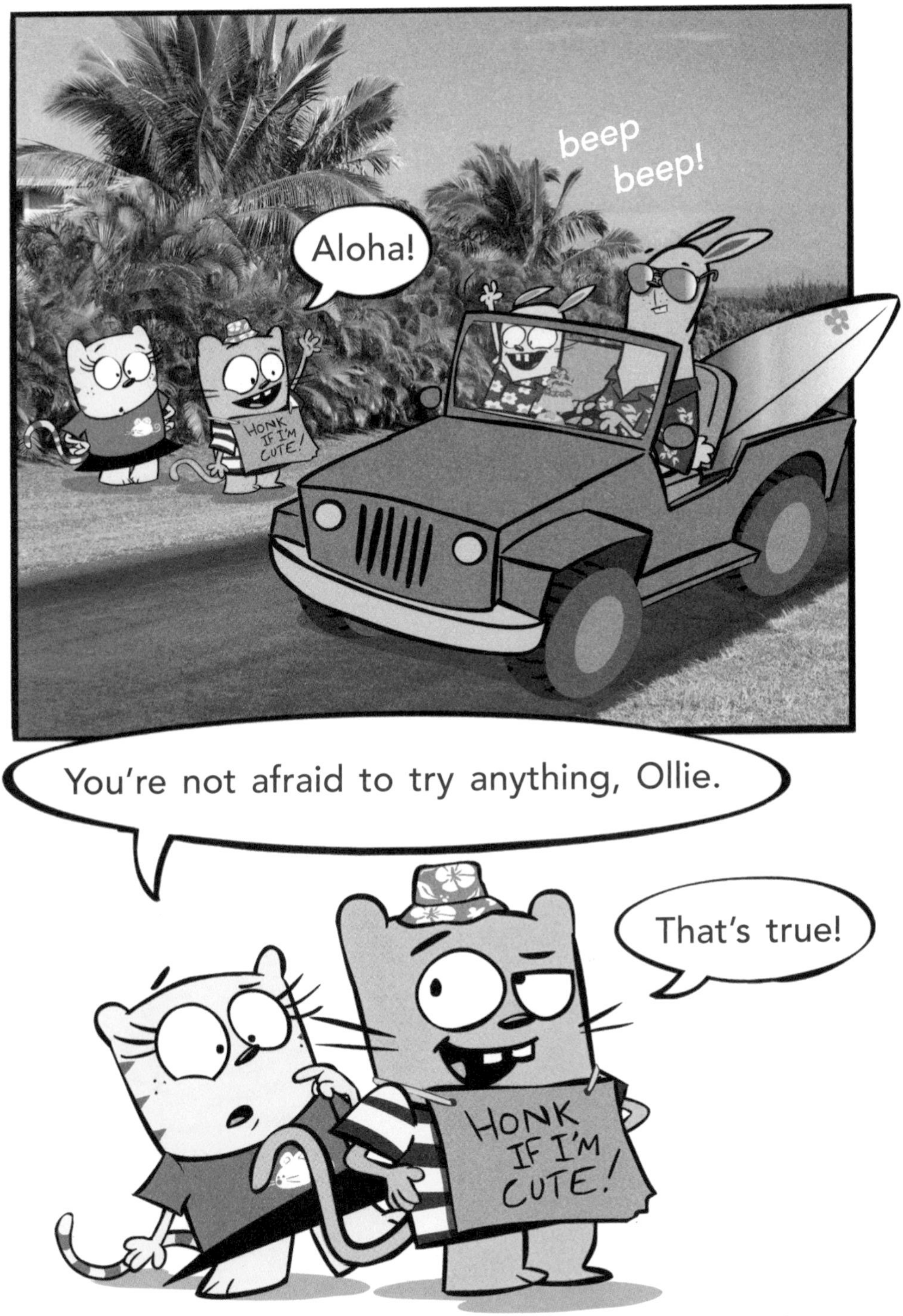
beep
beep!
Aloha!
HONK IF I'M CUTE!
You're not afraid to try anything, Ollie.
That's true!
HONK IF I'M CUTE!

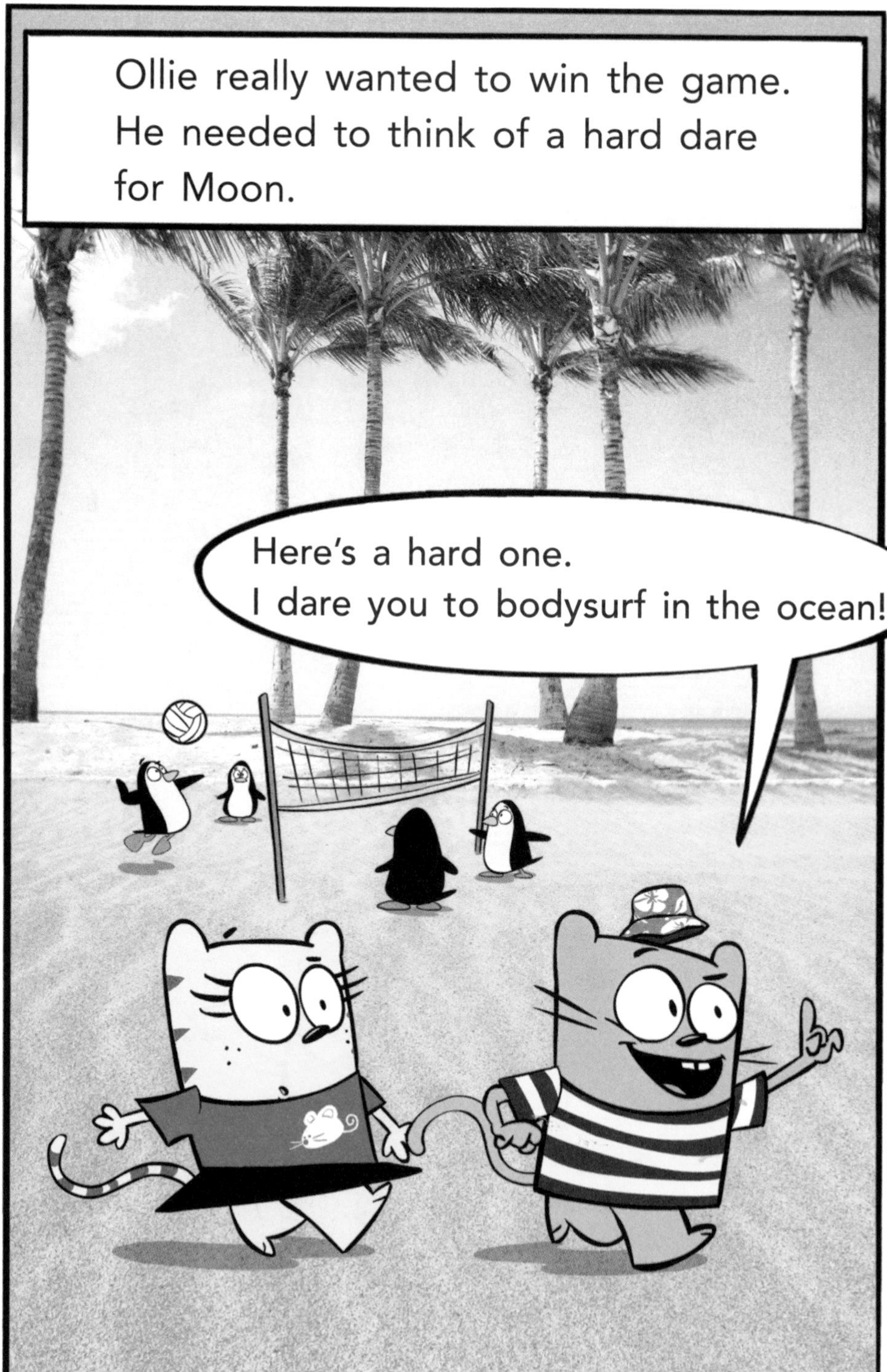
Ollie really wanted to win the game. He needed to think of a hard dare for Moon.
Here's a hard one. I dare you to bodysurf in the ocean!

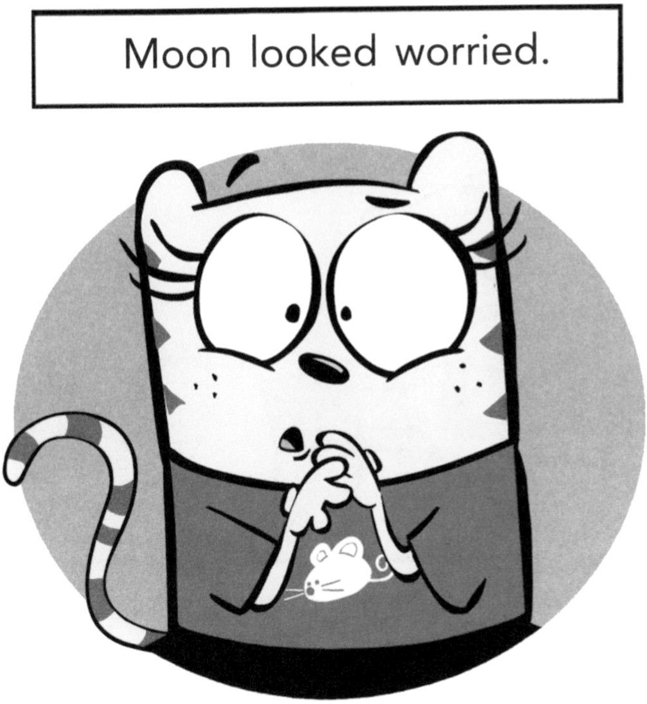
Moon looked worried.

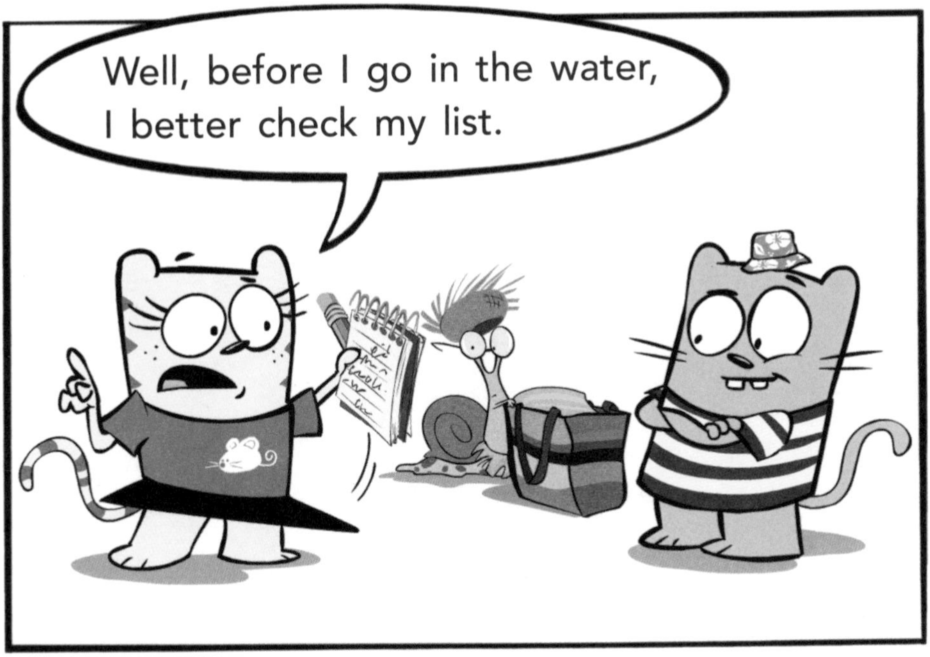
Well, before I go in the water,
I better check my list.

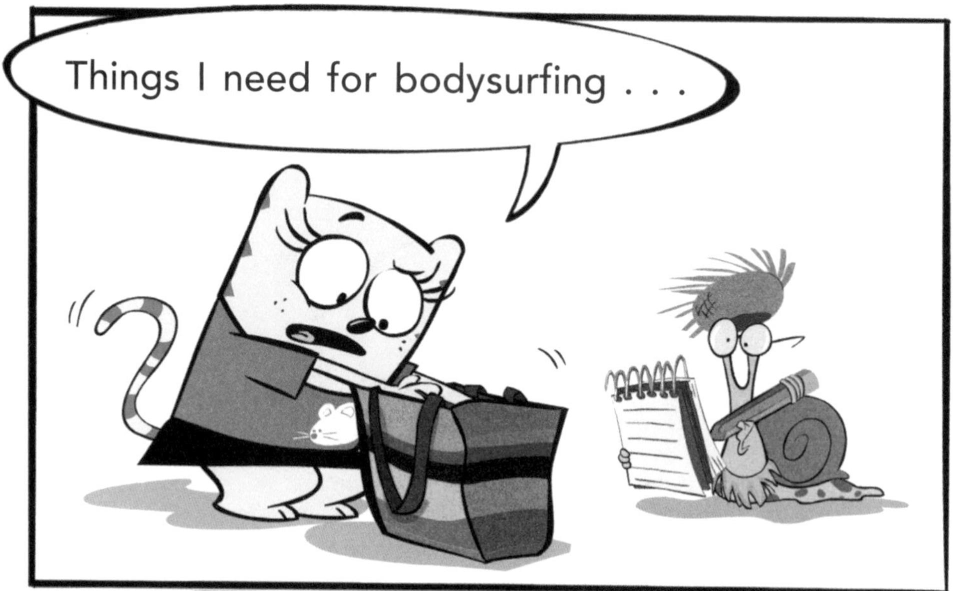
Things I need for bodysurfing . . .

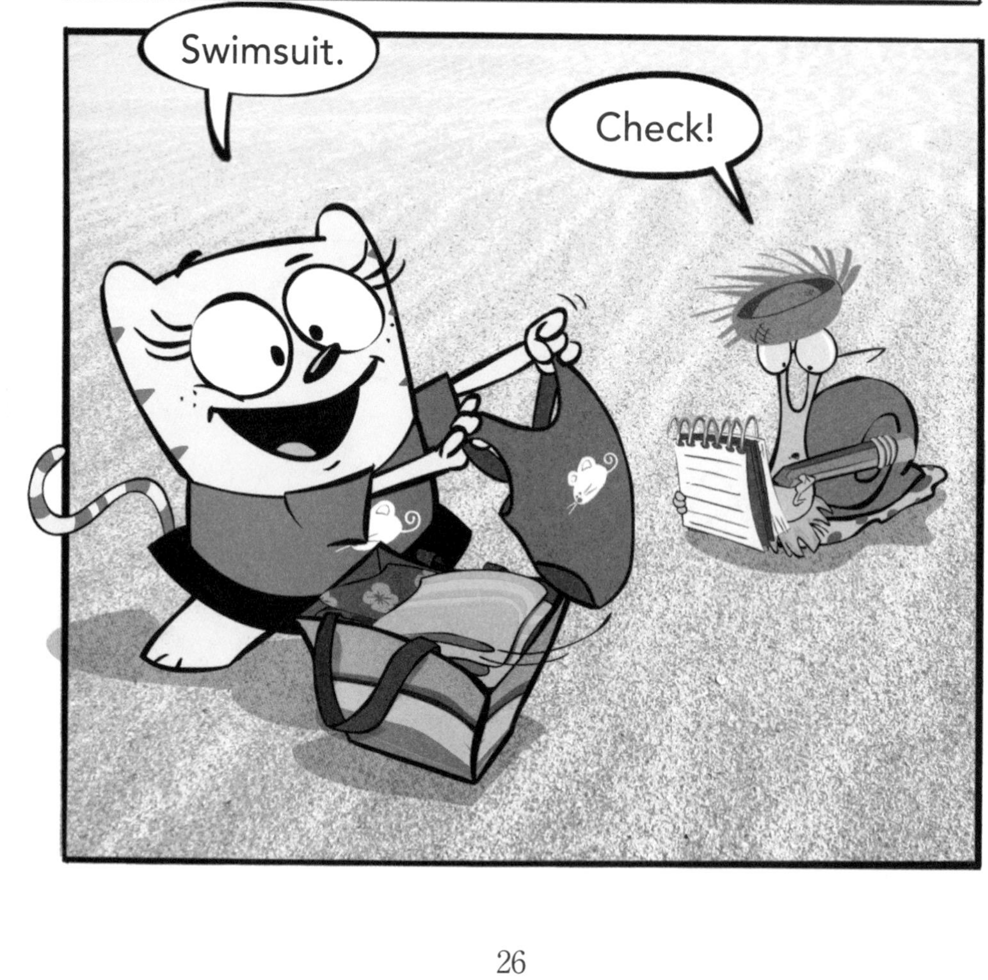
Swimsuit.
Check!

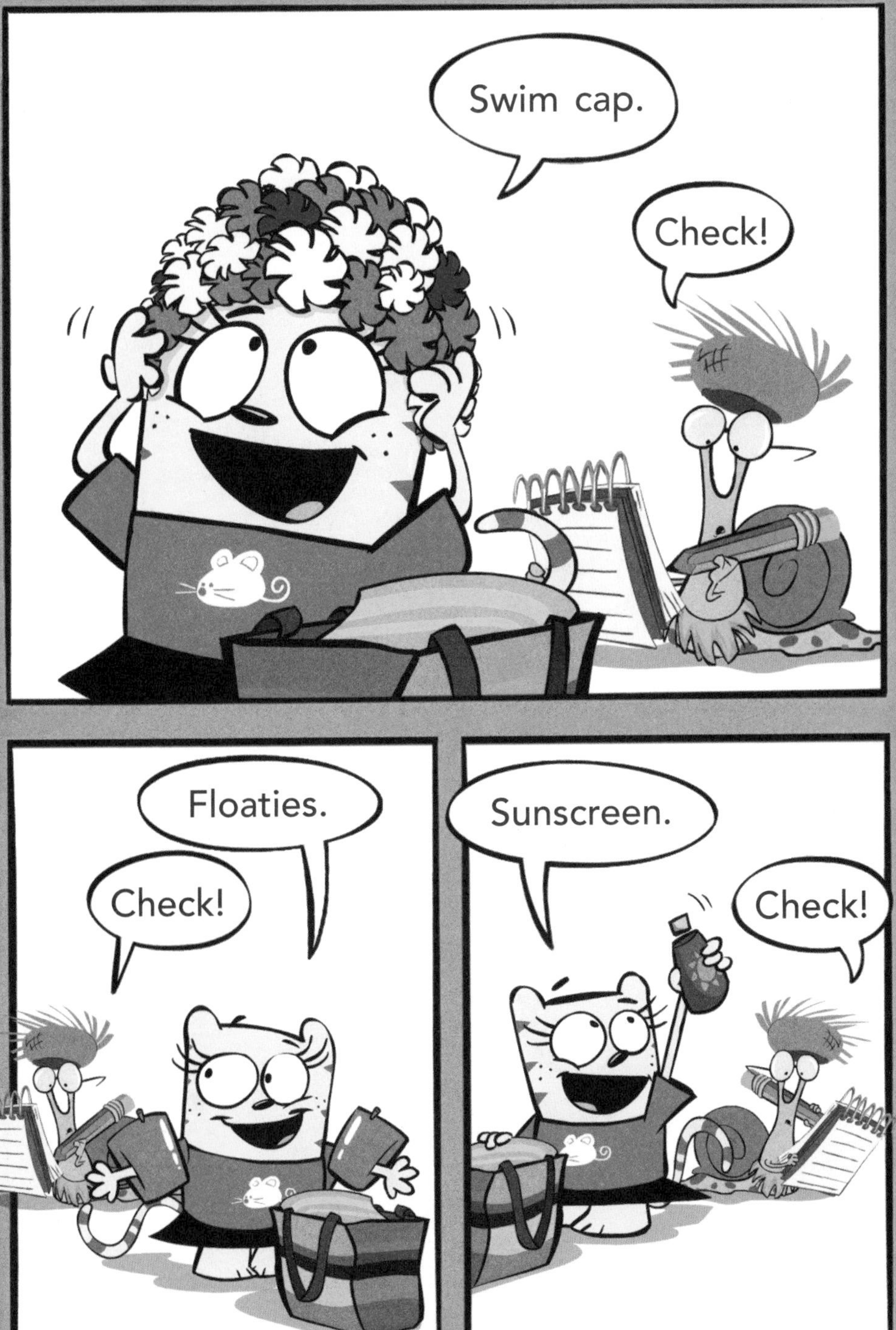

Swim cap.
Check!
Floaties.
Check!
Sunscreen.
Check!

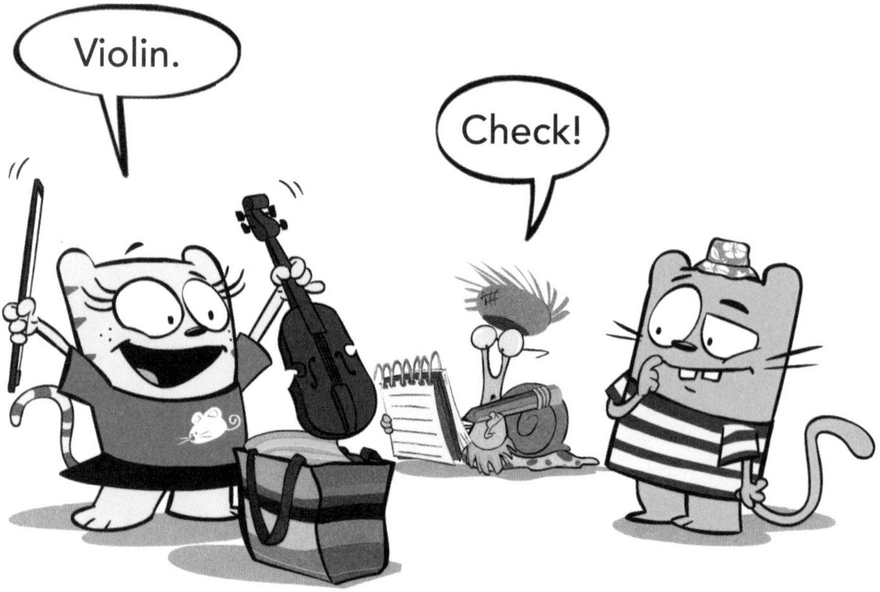
Violin.
Check!

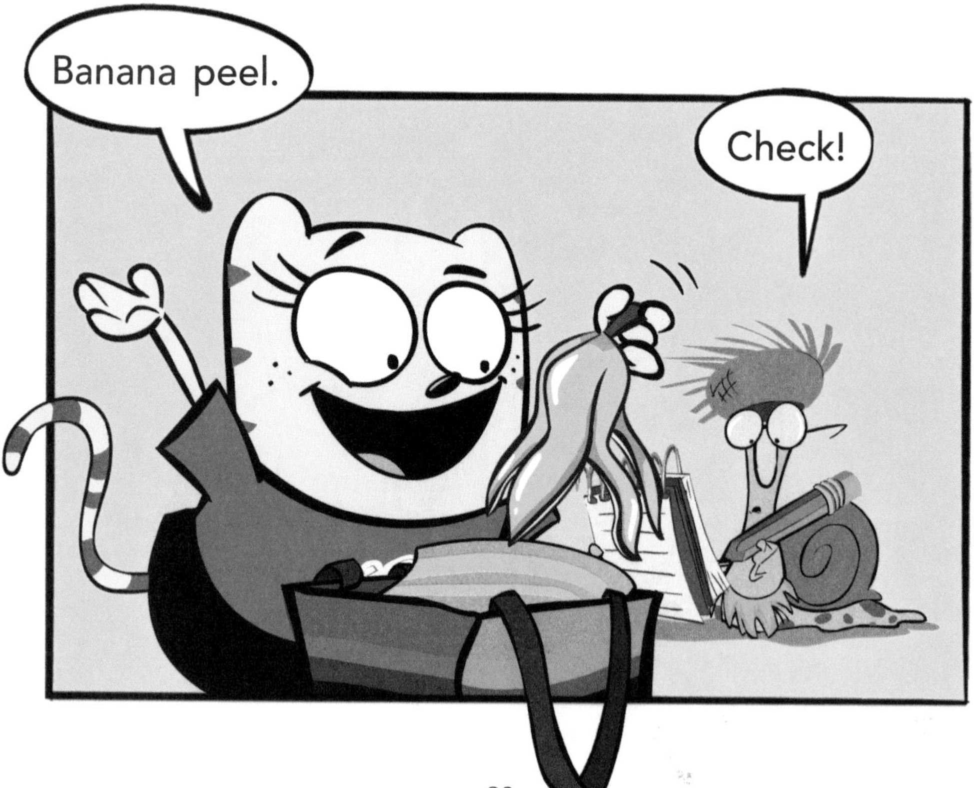
Banana peel.
Check!

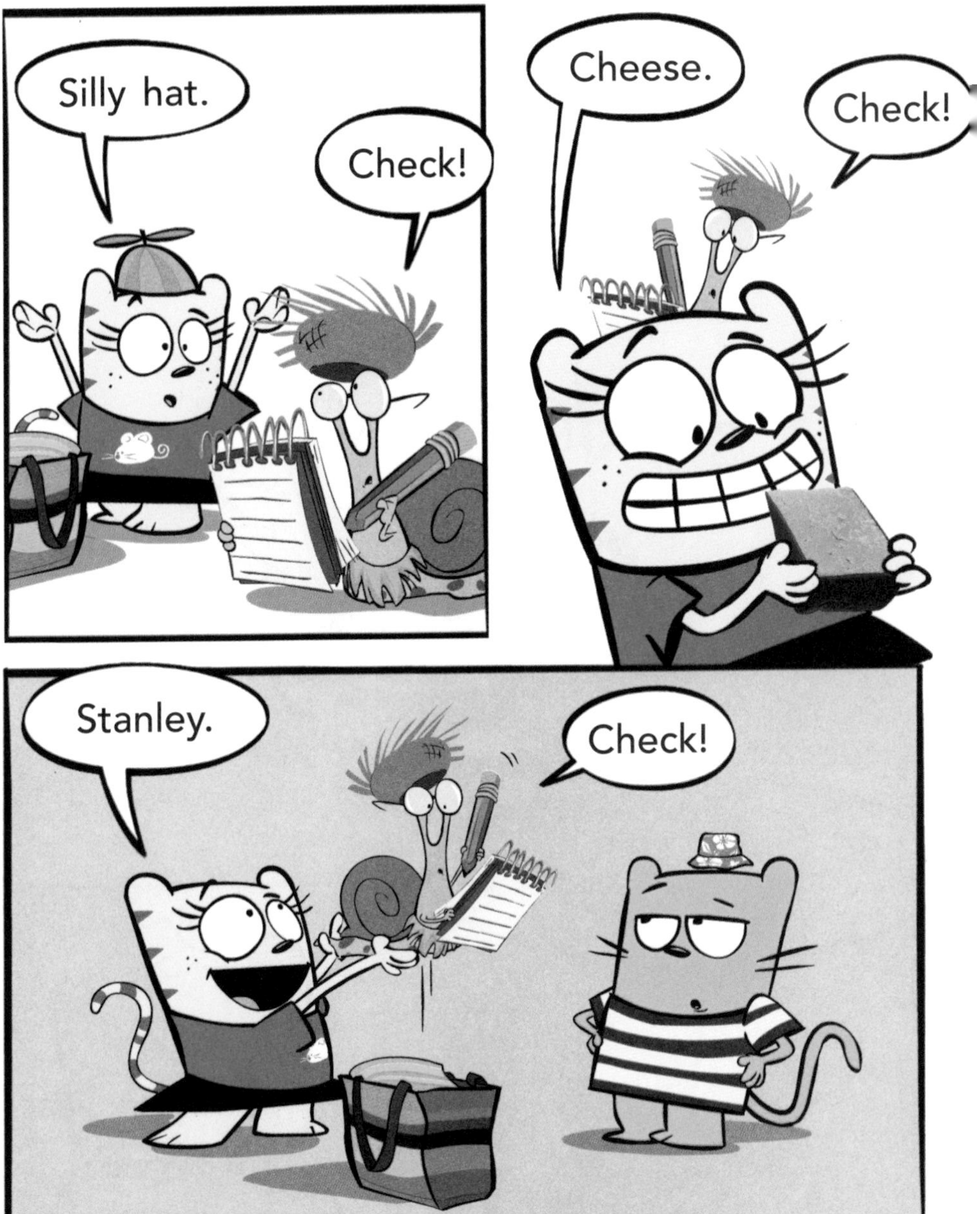
Silly hat.
Check!
Cheese.
Check!
Stanley.
Check!

Ollie thought Moon's checklist would never end.
Could Moon be stalling?

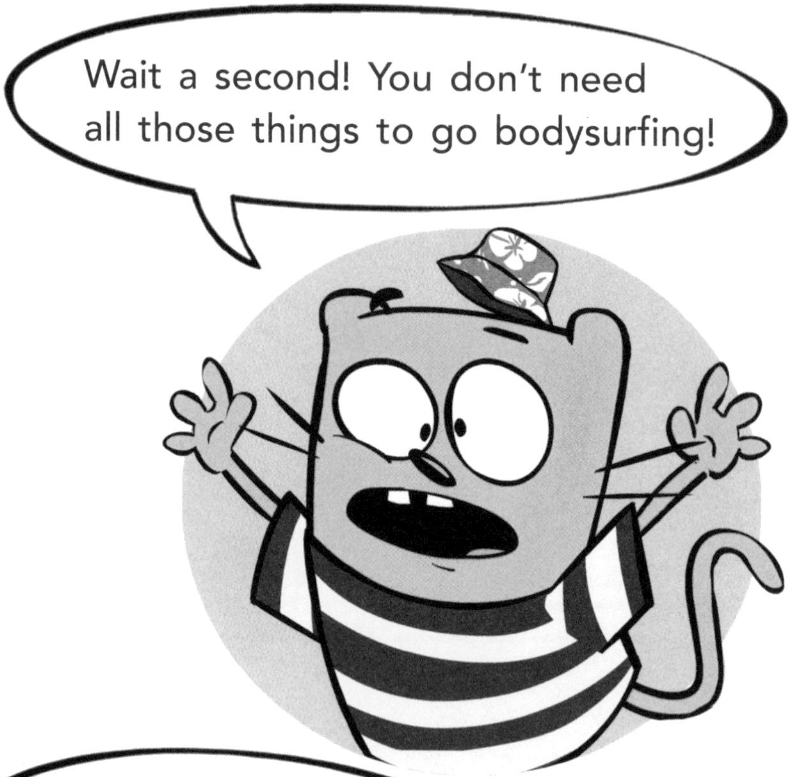
Wait a second! You don't need all those things to go bodysurfing!

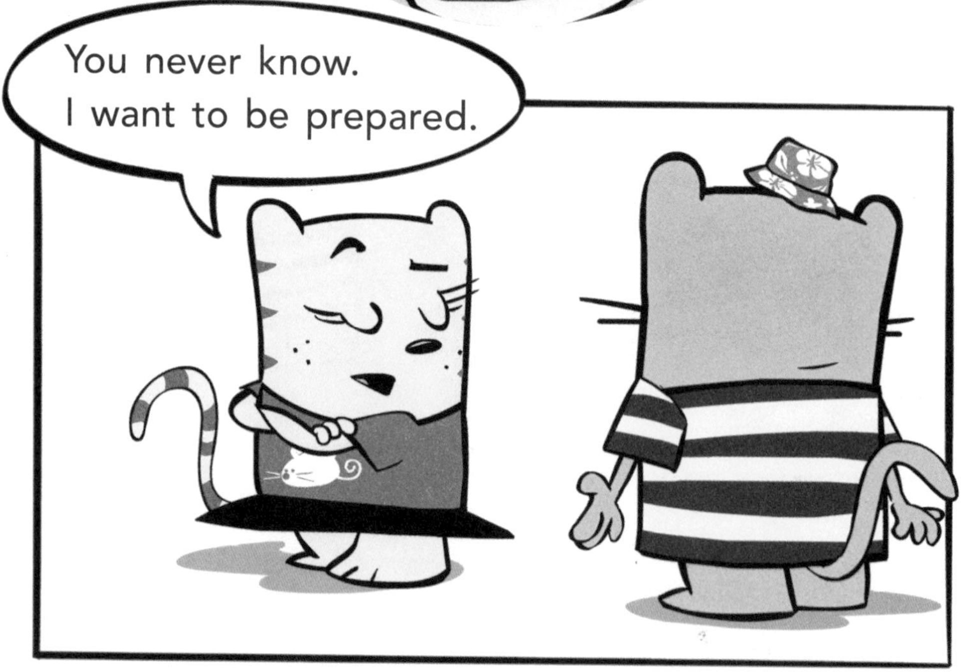
You never know. I want to be prepared.

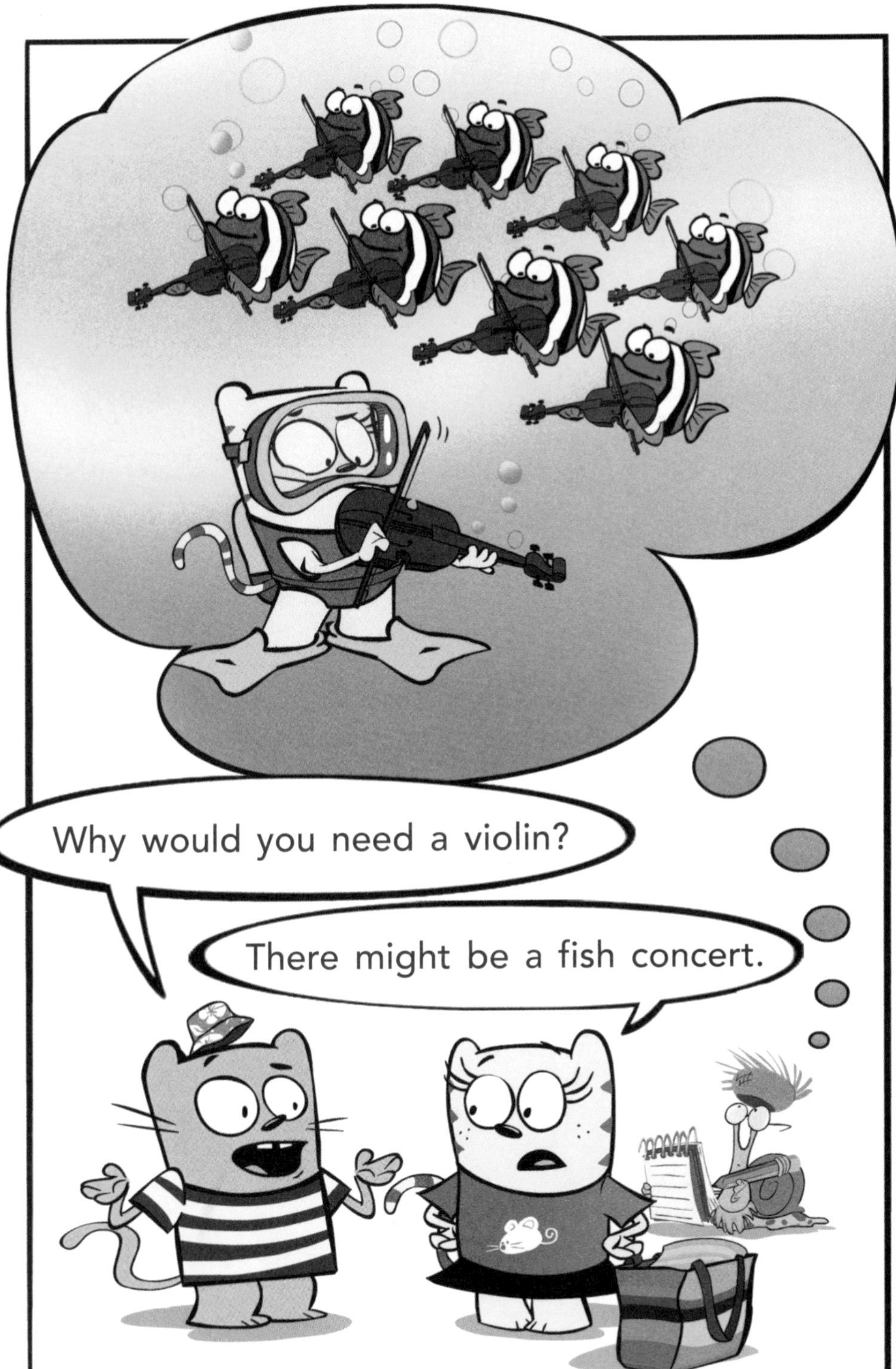
Why would you need a violin?
There might be a fish concert.

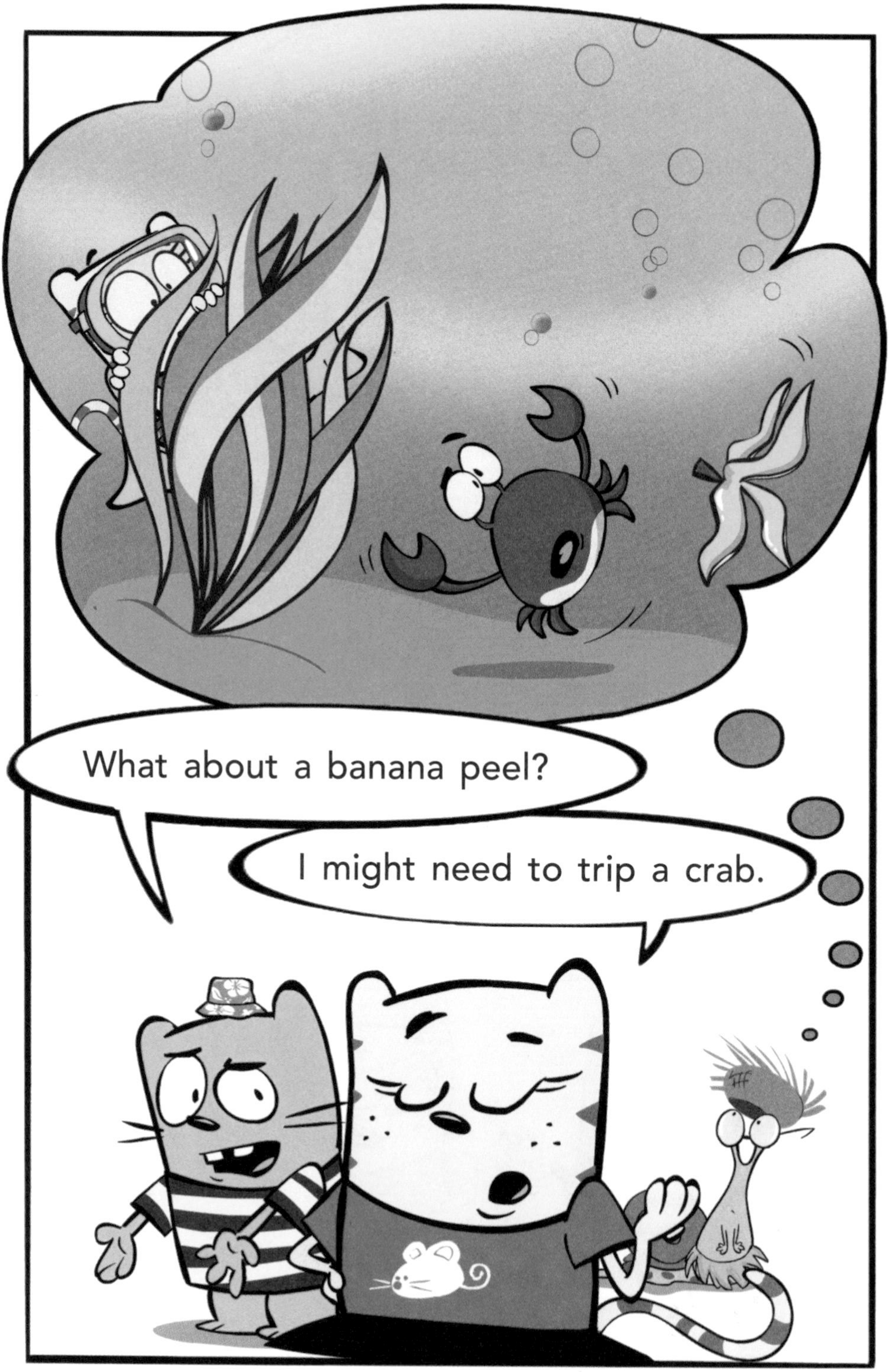
What about a banana peel?
I might need to trip a crab.

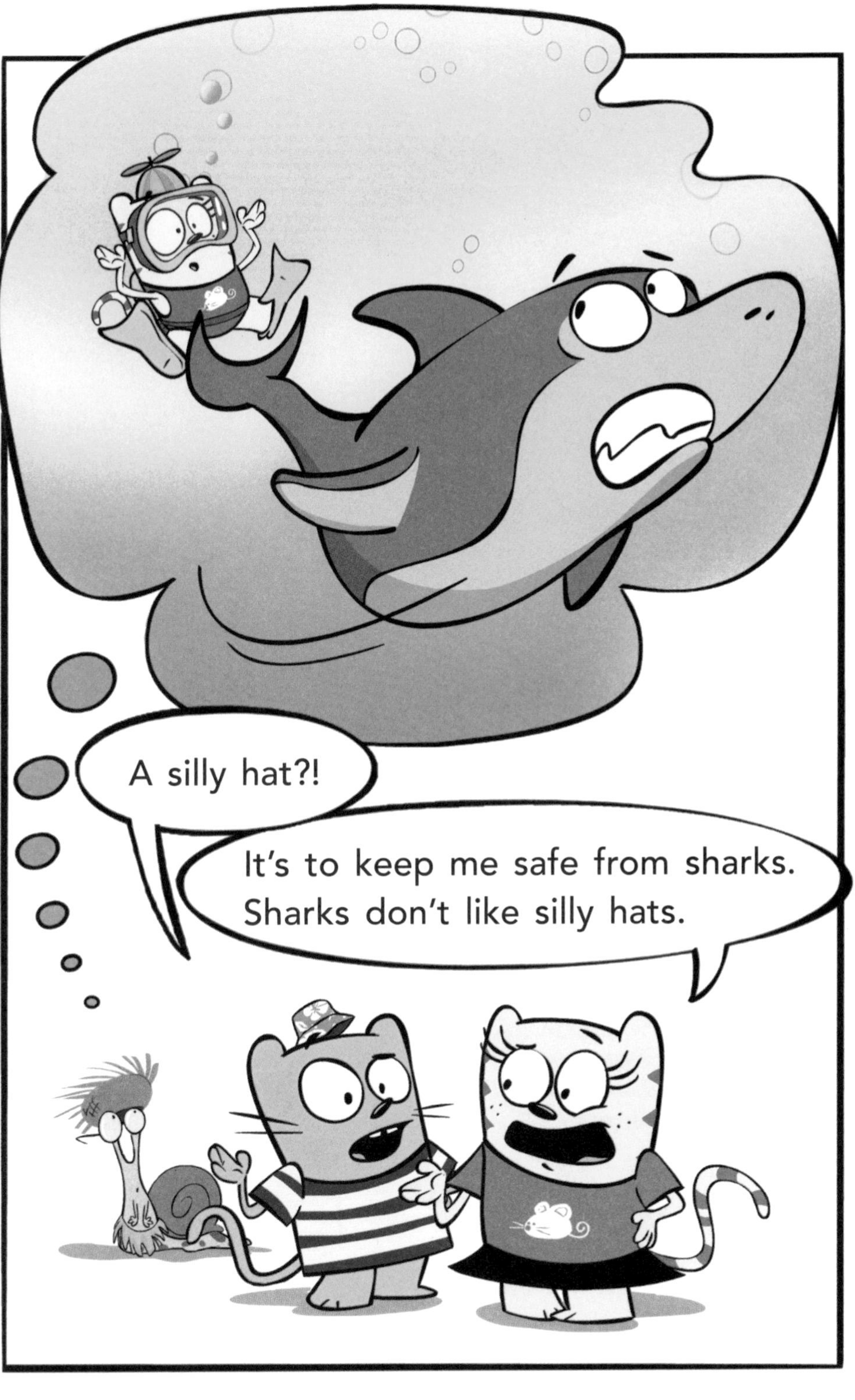
A silly hat?!
It's to keep me safe from sharks. Sharks don't like silly hats.

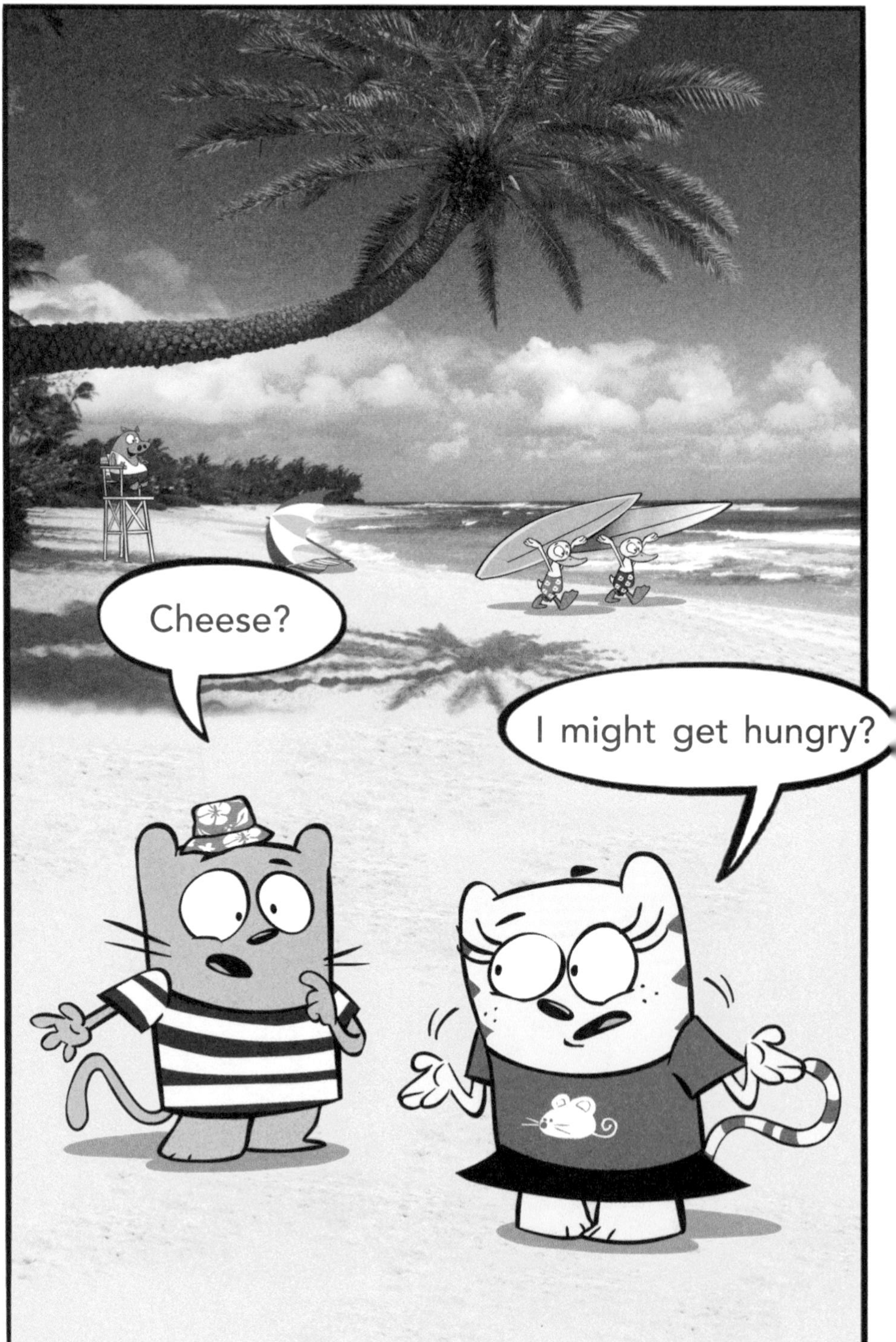
Cheese?
I might get hungry?

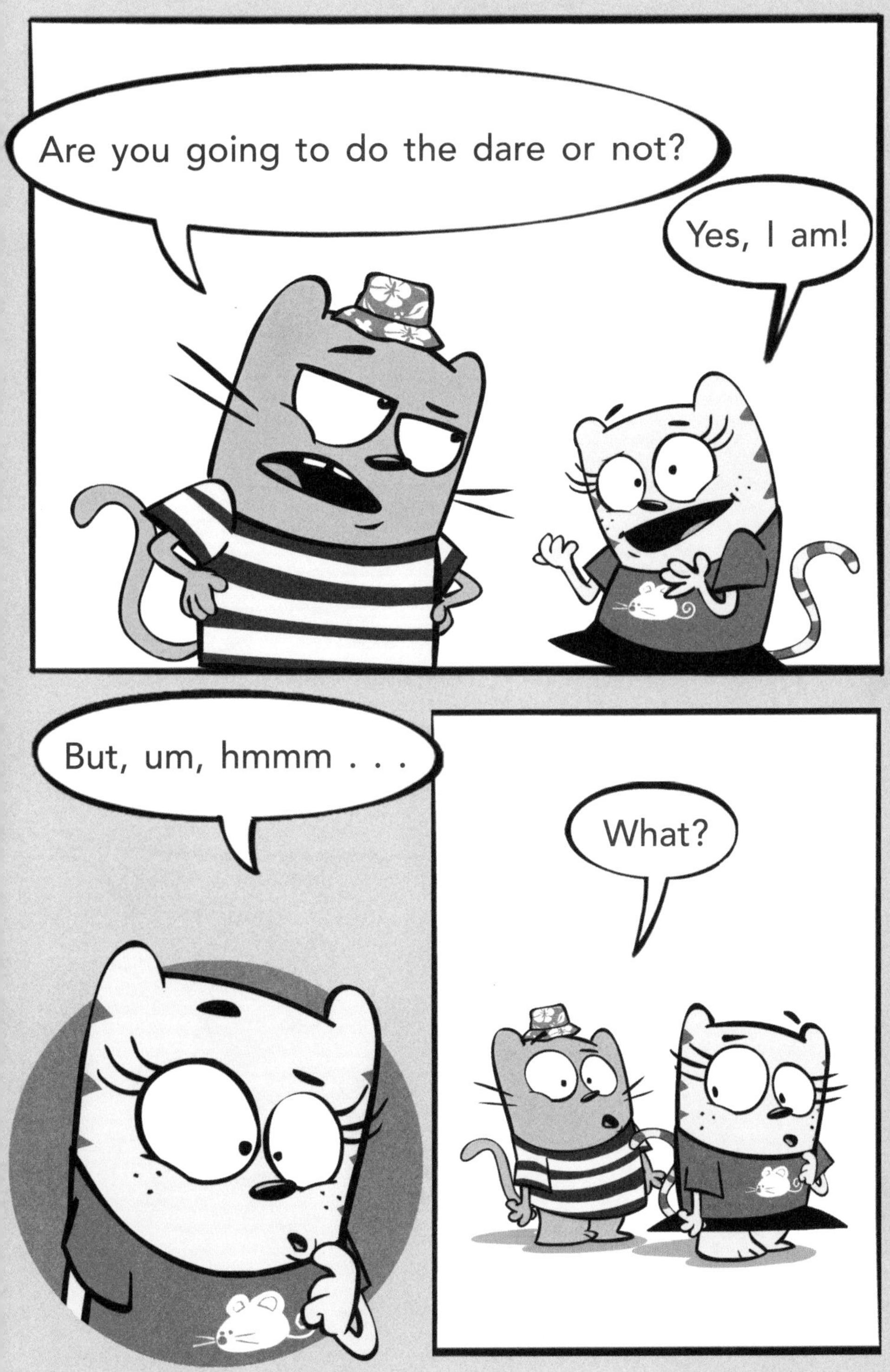
Are you going to do the dare or not?
Yes, I am!
But, um, hmmm . . .
What?

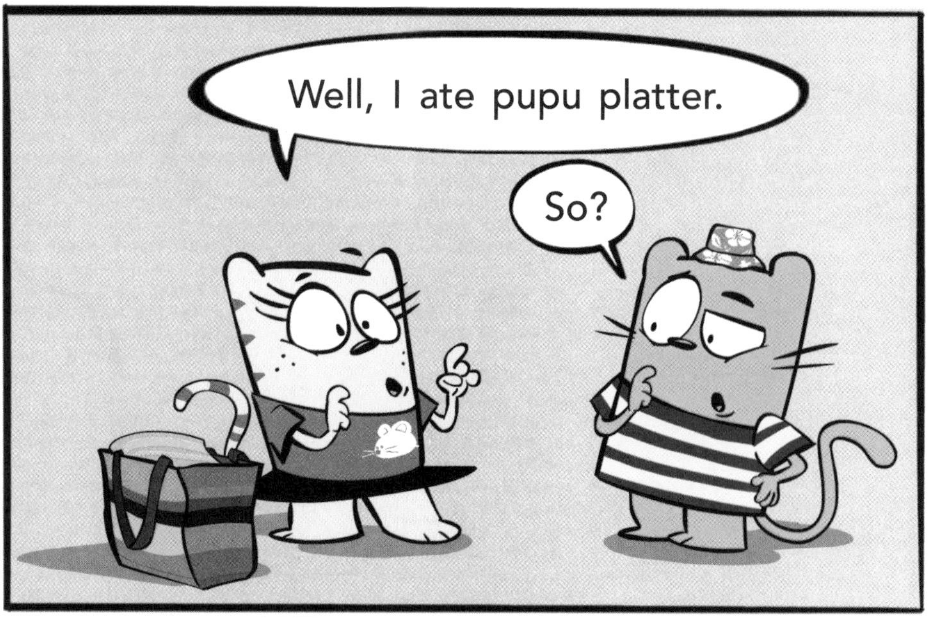
Well, I ate pupu platter.
So?

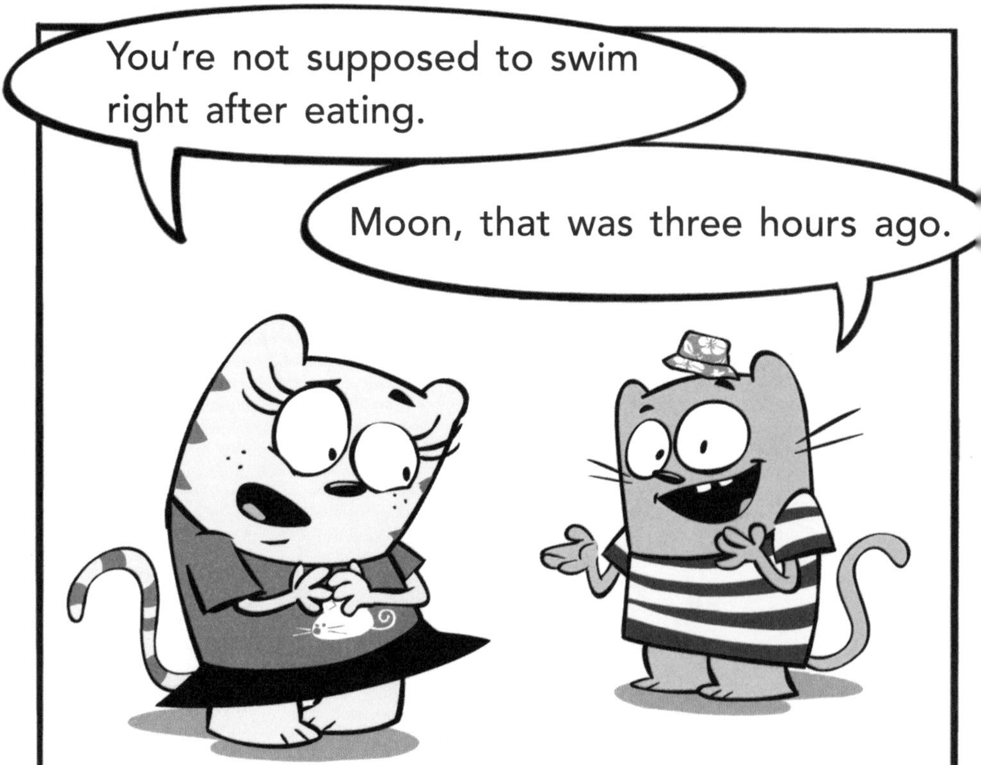
You're not supposed to swim right after eating.
Moon, that was three hours ago.

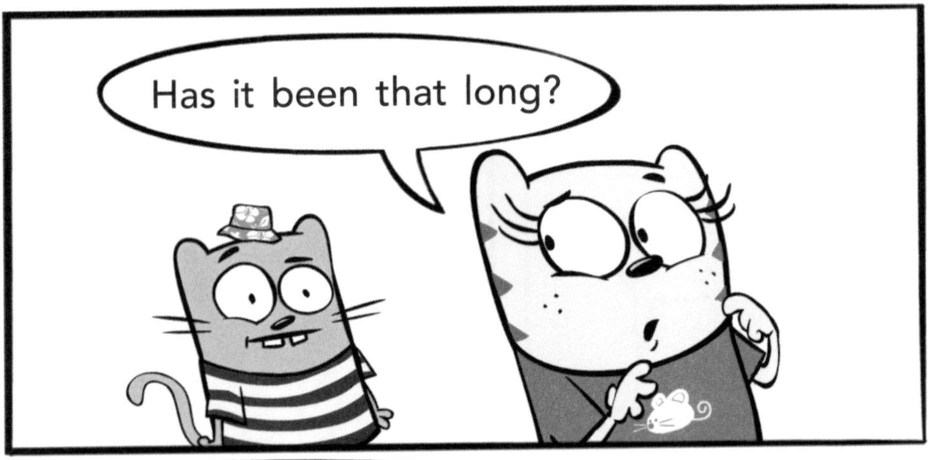
Has it been that long?

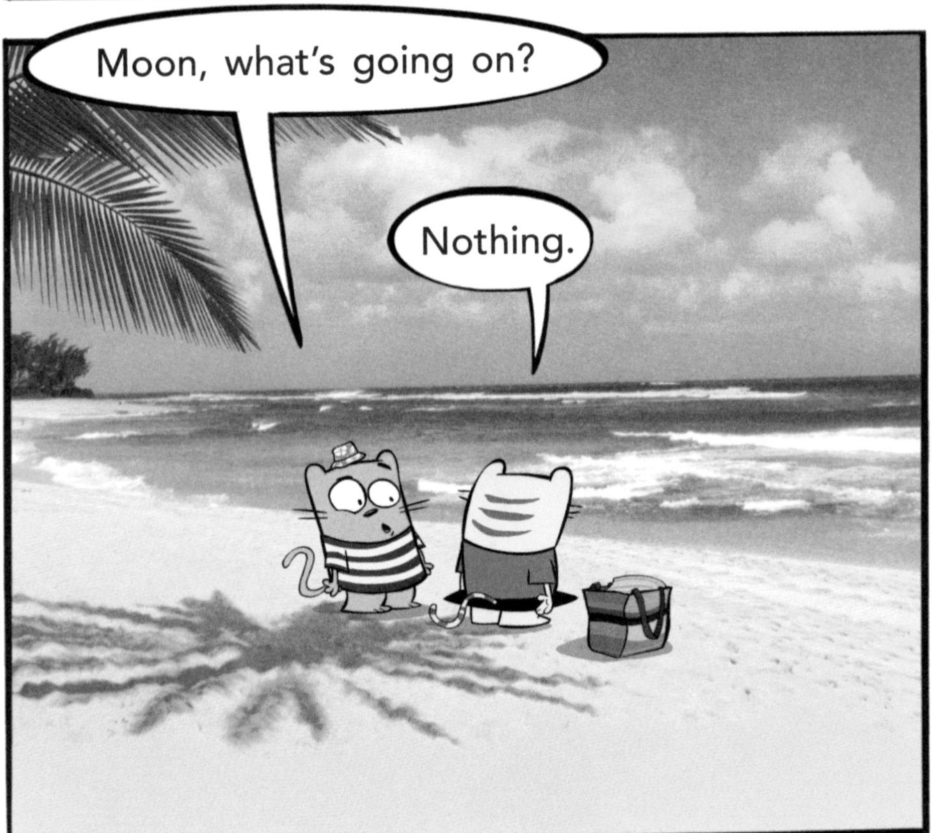
Moon, what's going on?
Nothing.

Ollie wondered if Moon
was afraid to go in the ocean.

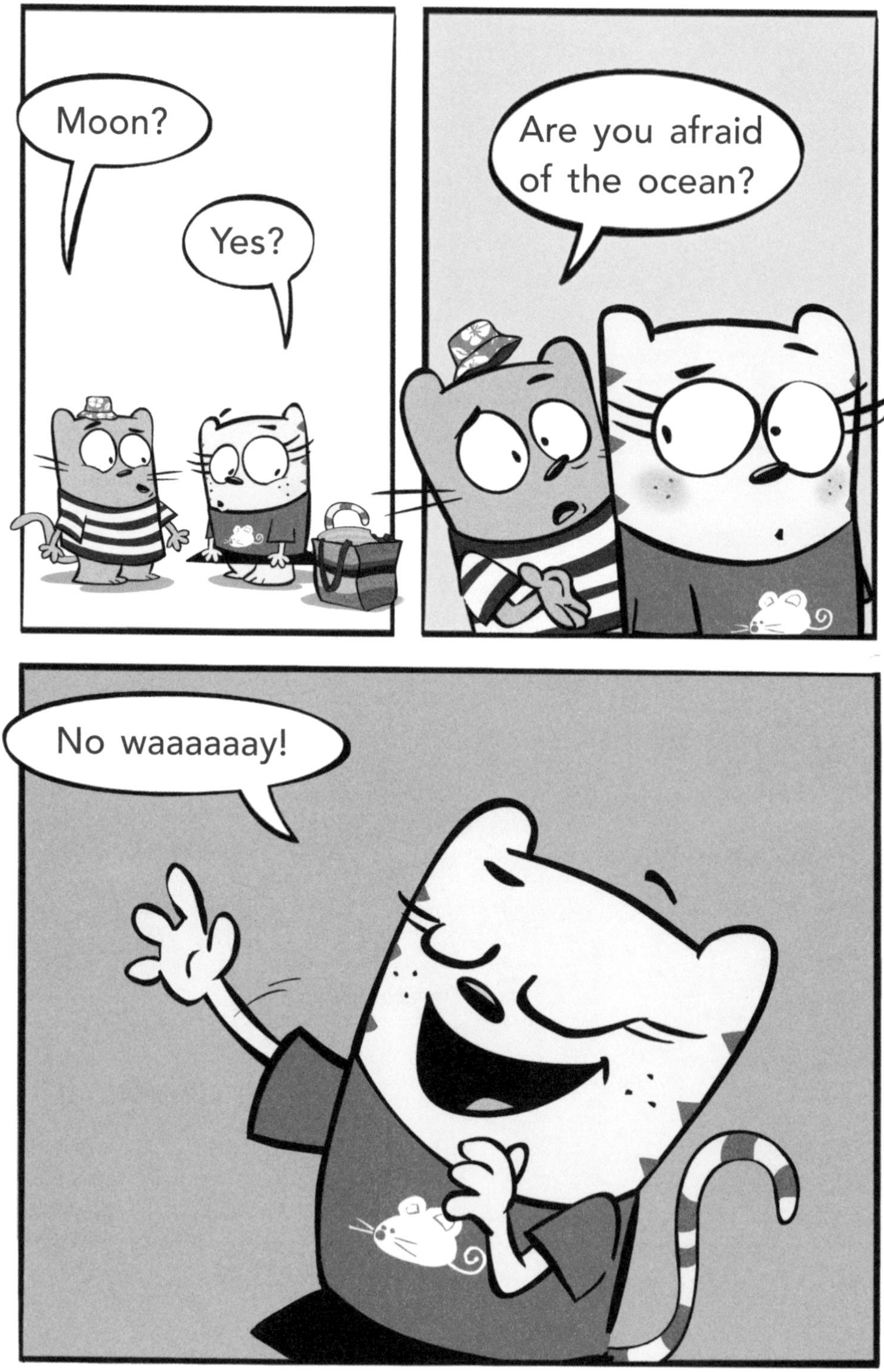
Moon?
Yes?
Are you afraid of the ocean?
No waaaaaay!

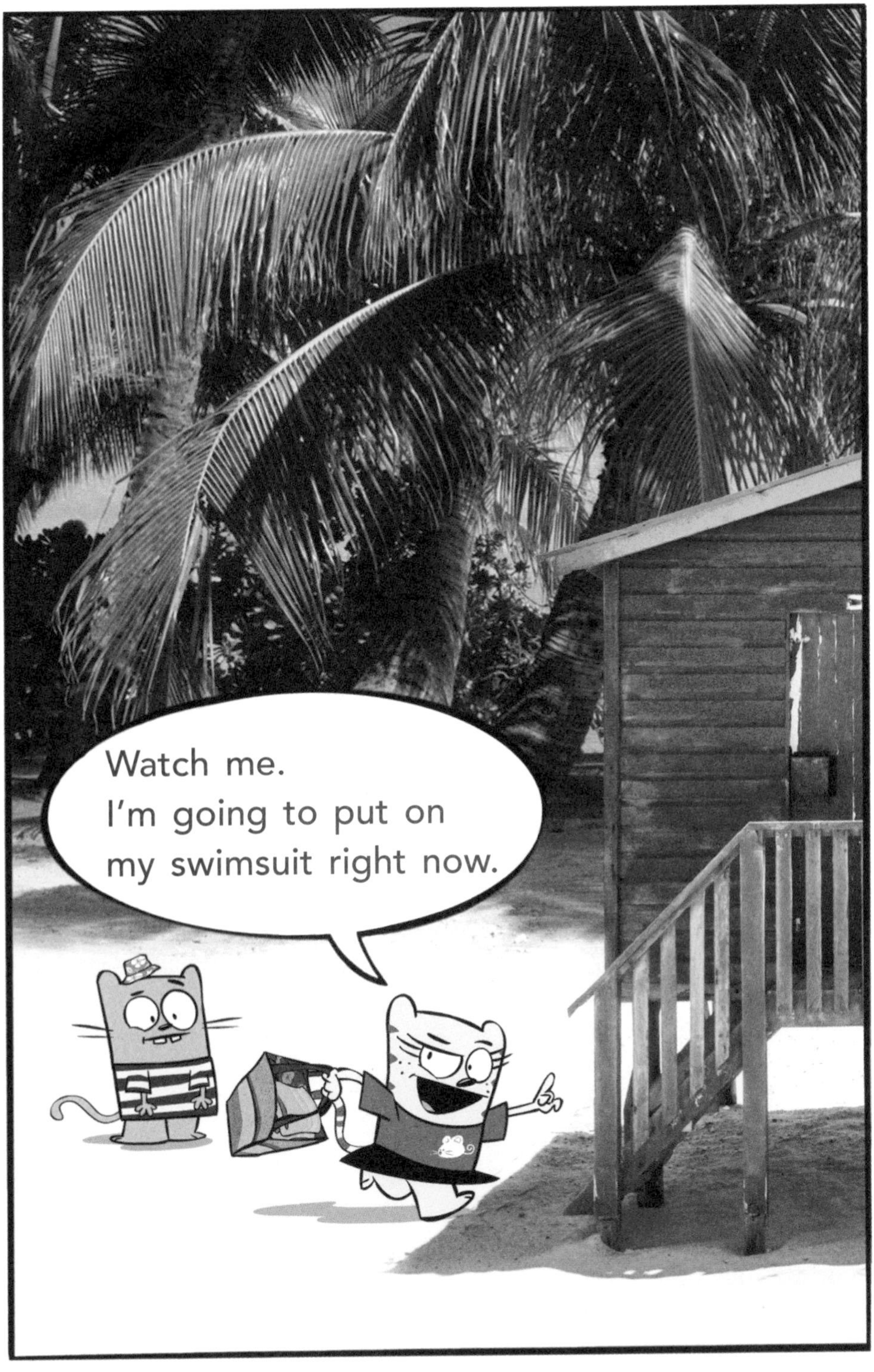
Watch me.
I'm going to put on
my swimsuit right now.

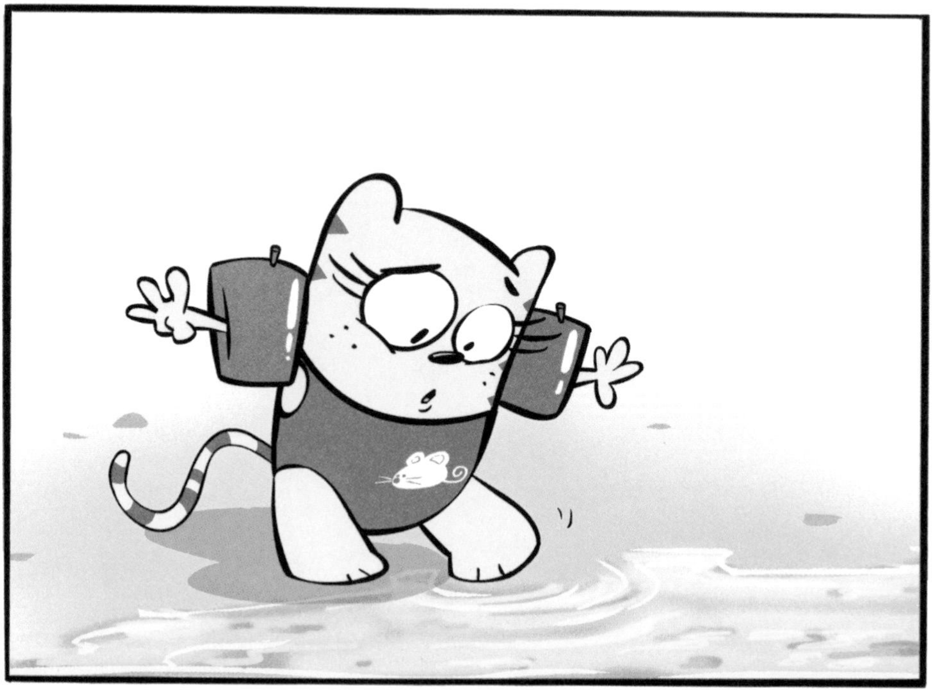

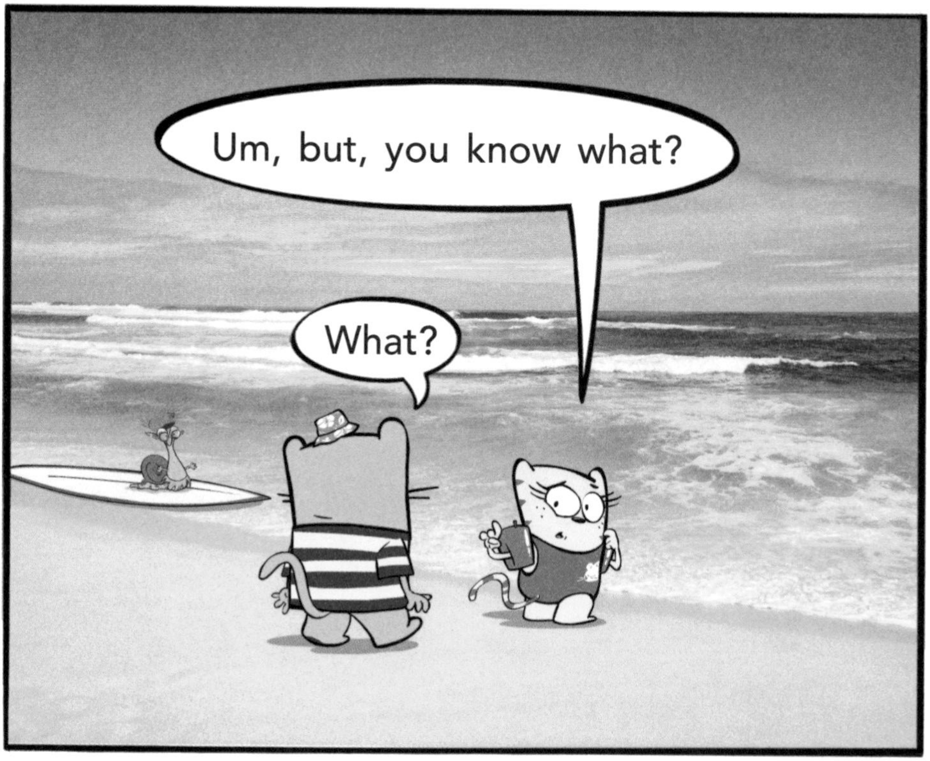
Um, but, you know what?
What?

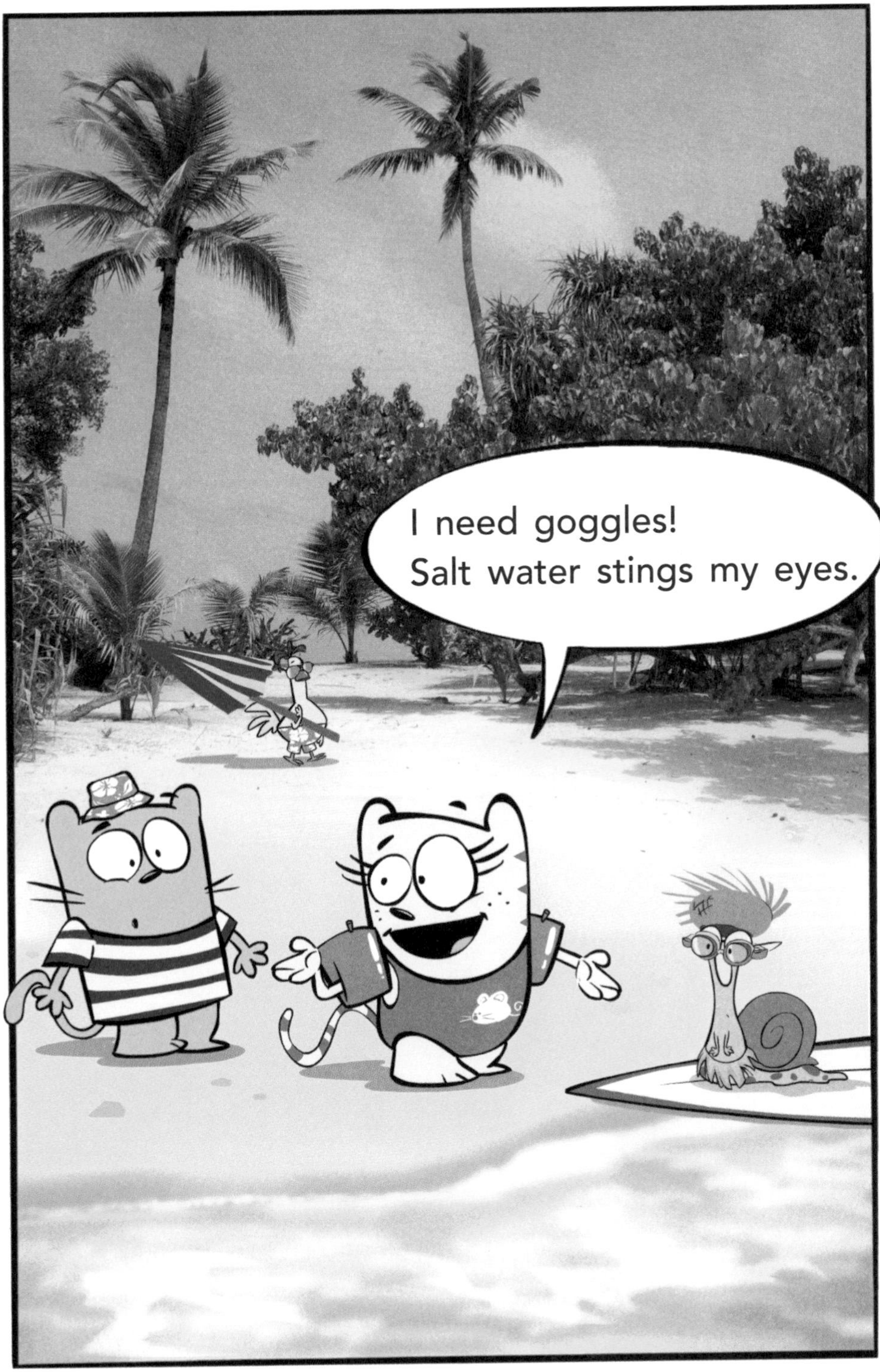
I need goggles!
Salt water stings my eyes.

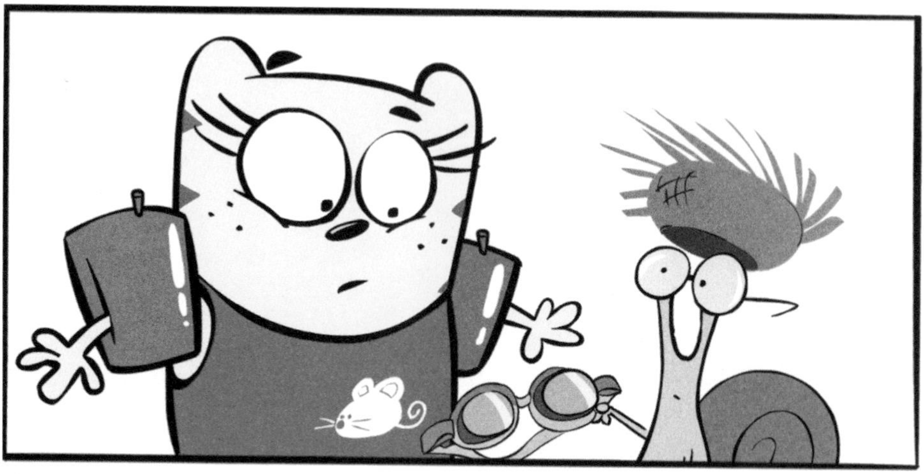

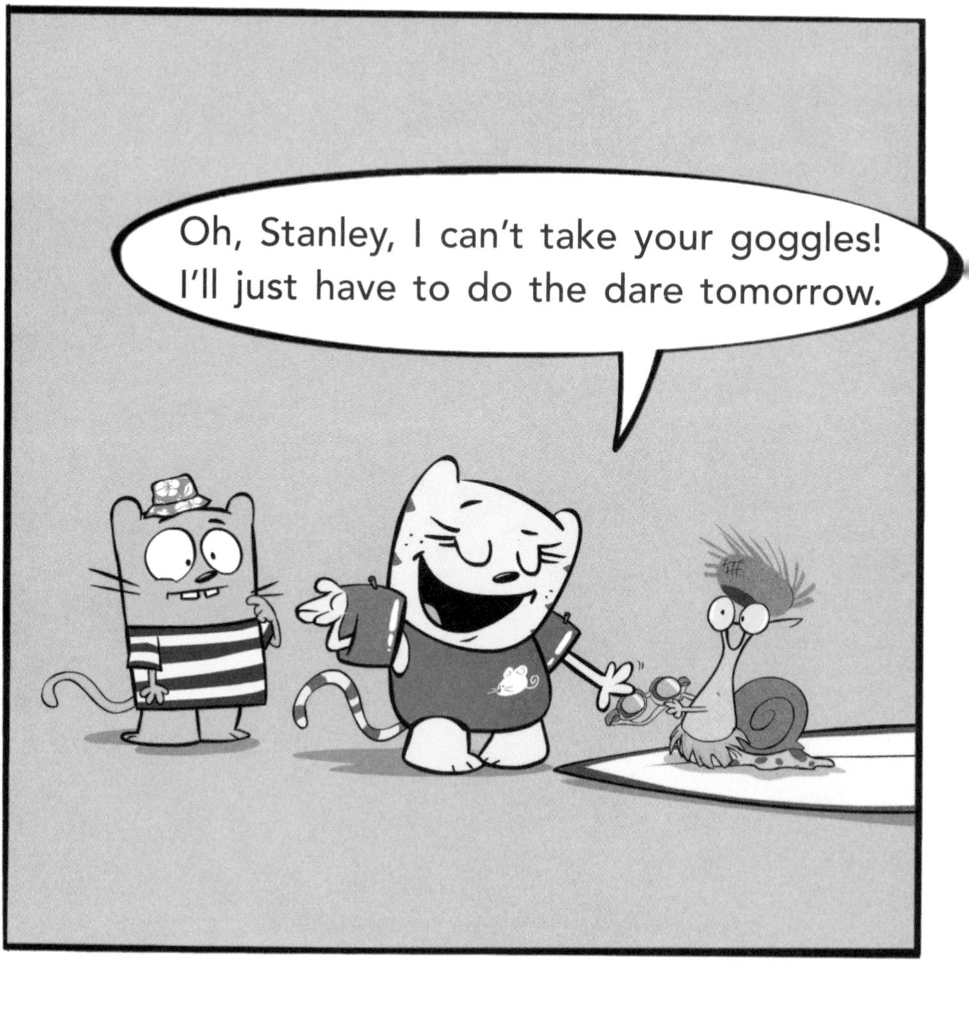
Oh, Stanley, I can't take your goggles! I'll just have to do the dare tomorrow.

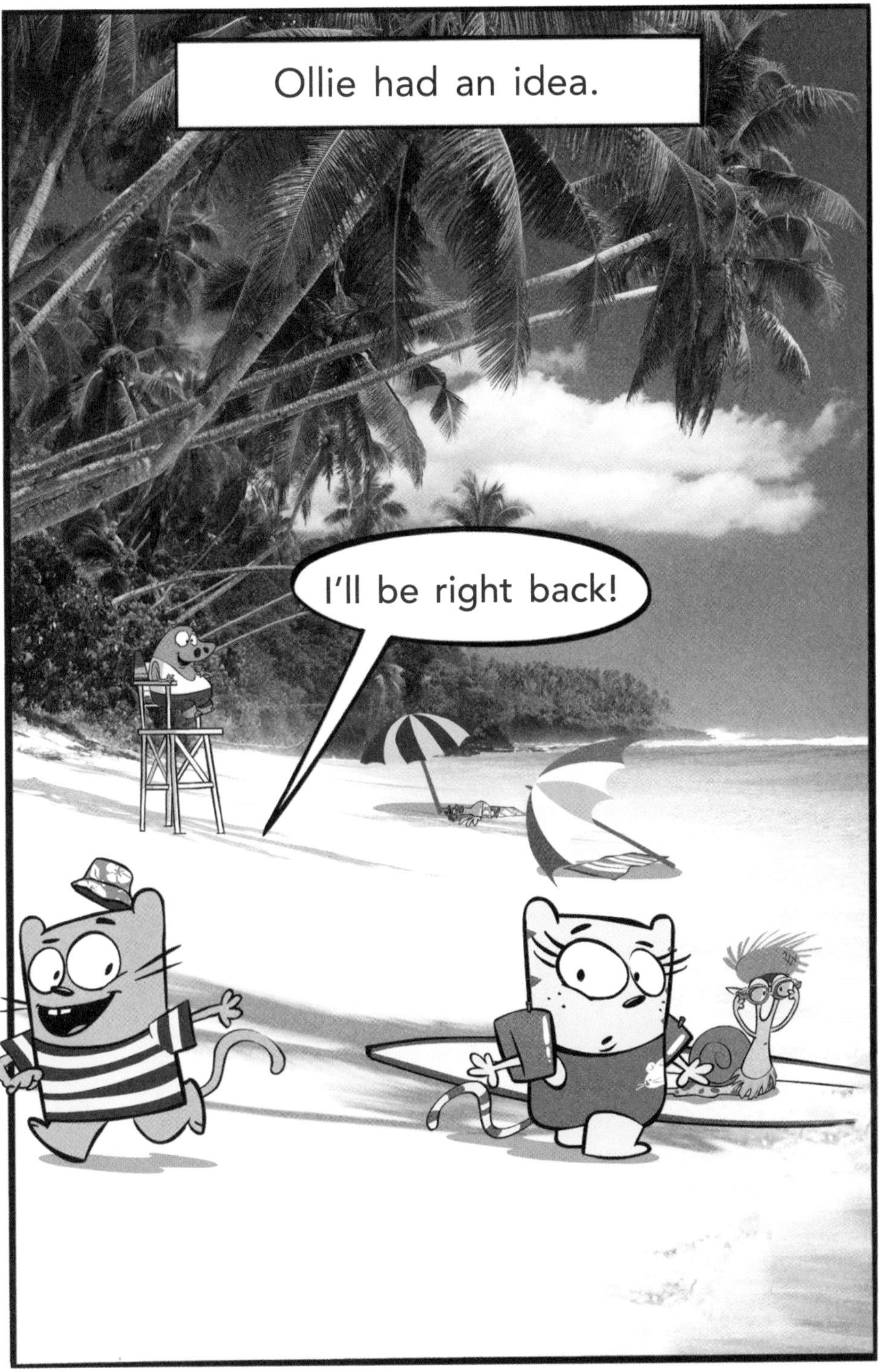
Ollie had an idea.
I'll be right back!

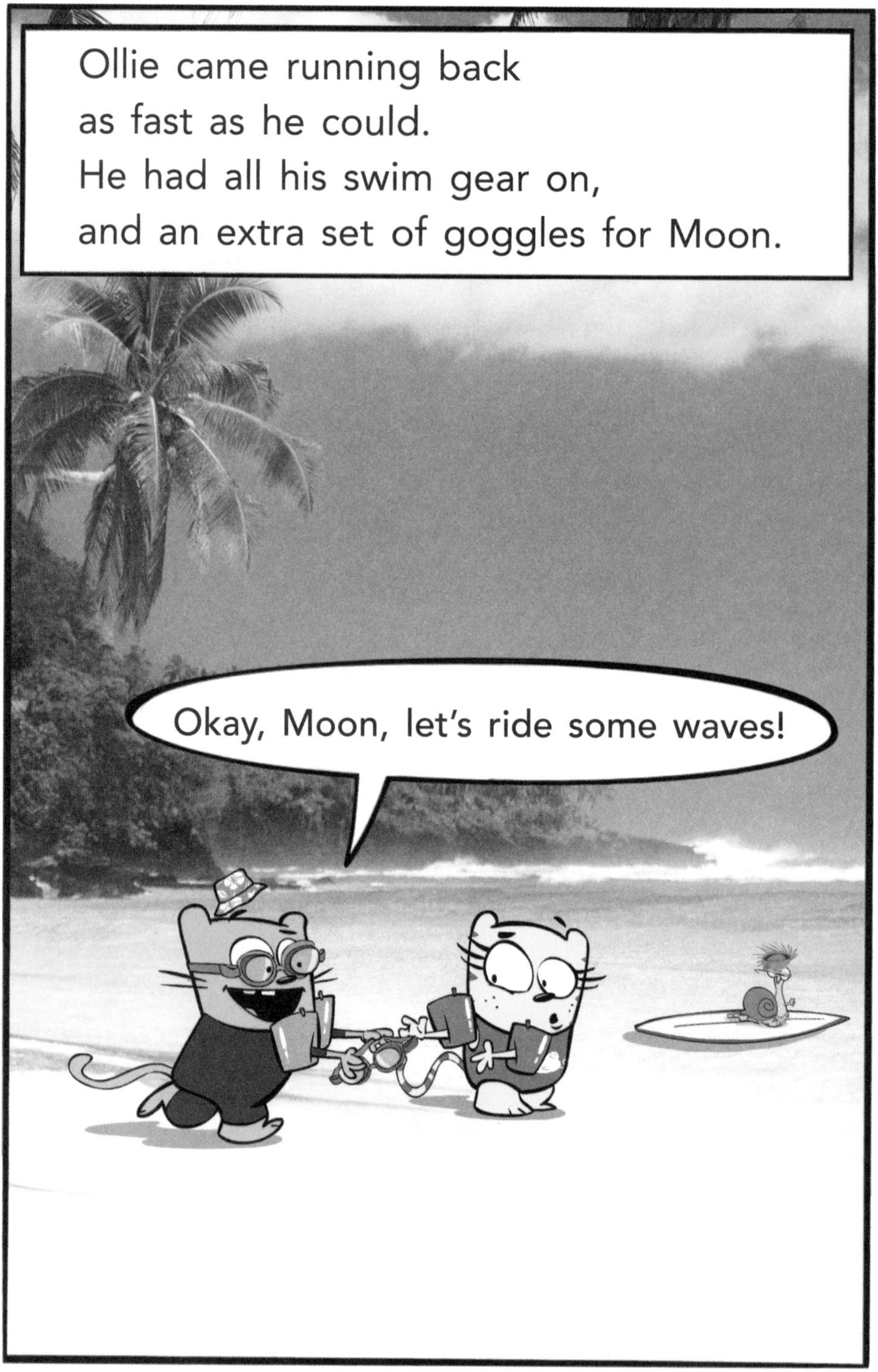
Ollie came running back
as fast as he could.
He had all his swim gear on,
and an extra set of goggles for Moon.
Okay, Moon, let's ride some waves!

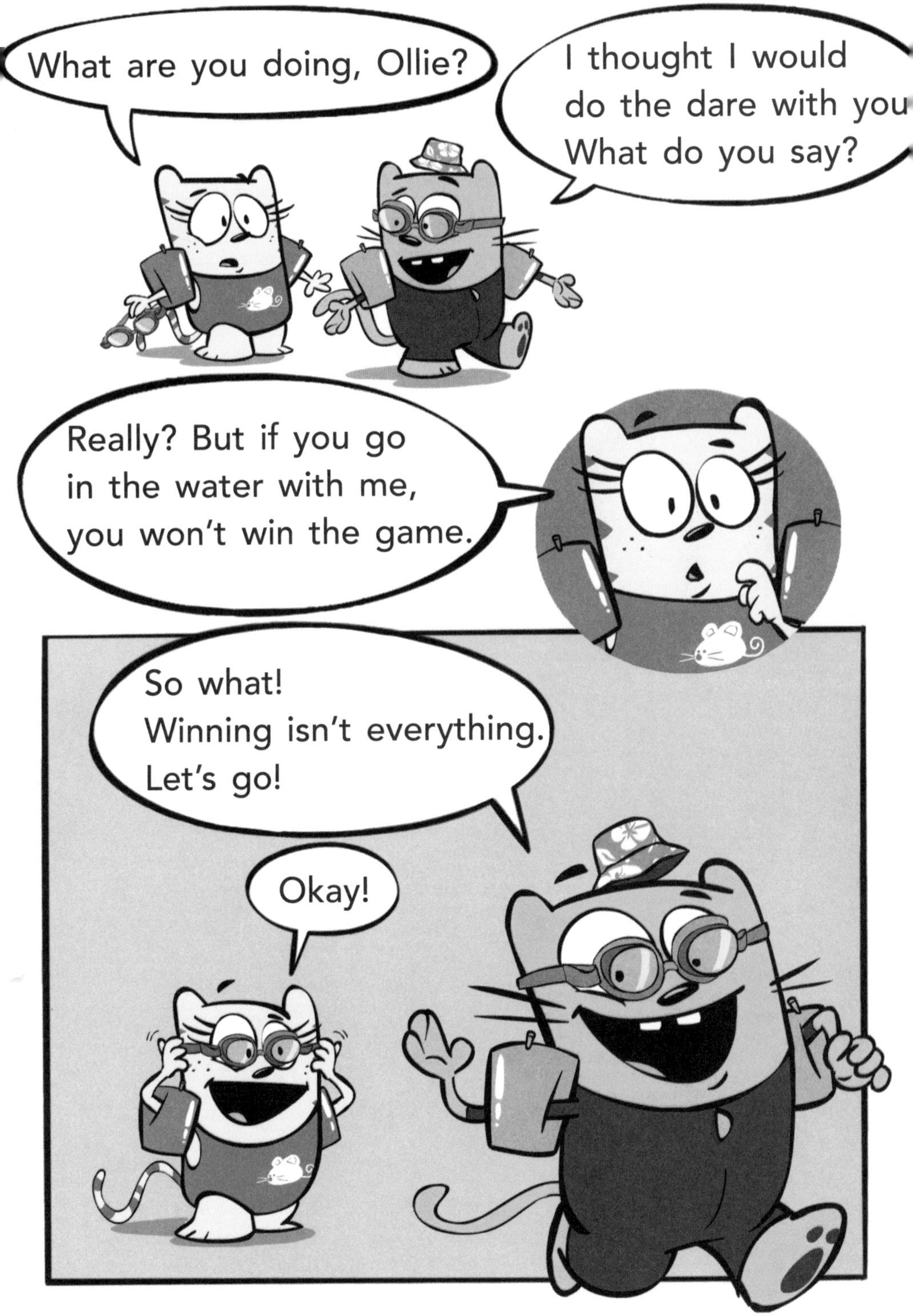
What are you doing, Ollie?
I thought I would do the dare with you What do you say?
Really? But if you go in the water with me, you won't win the game.
So what! Winning isn't everything. Let's go!
Okay!

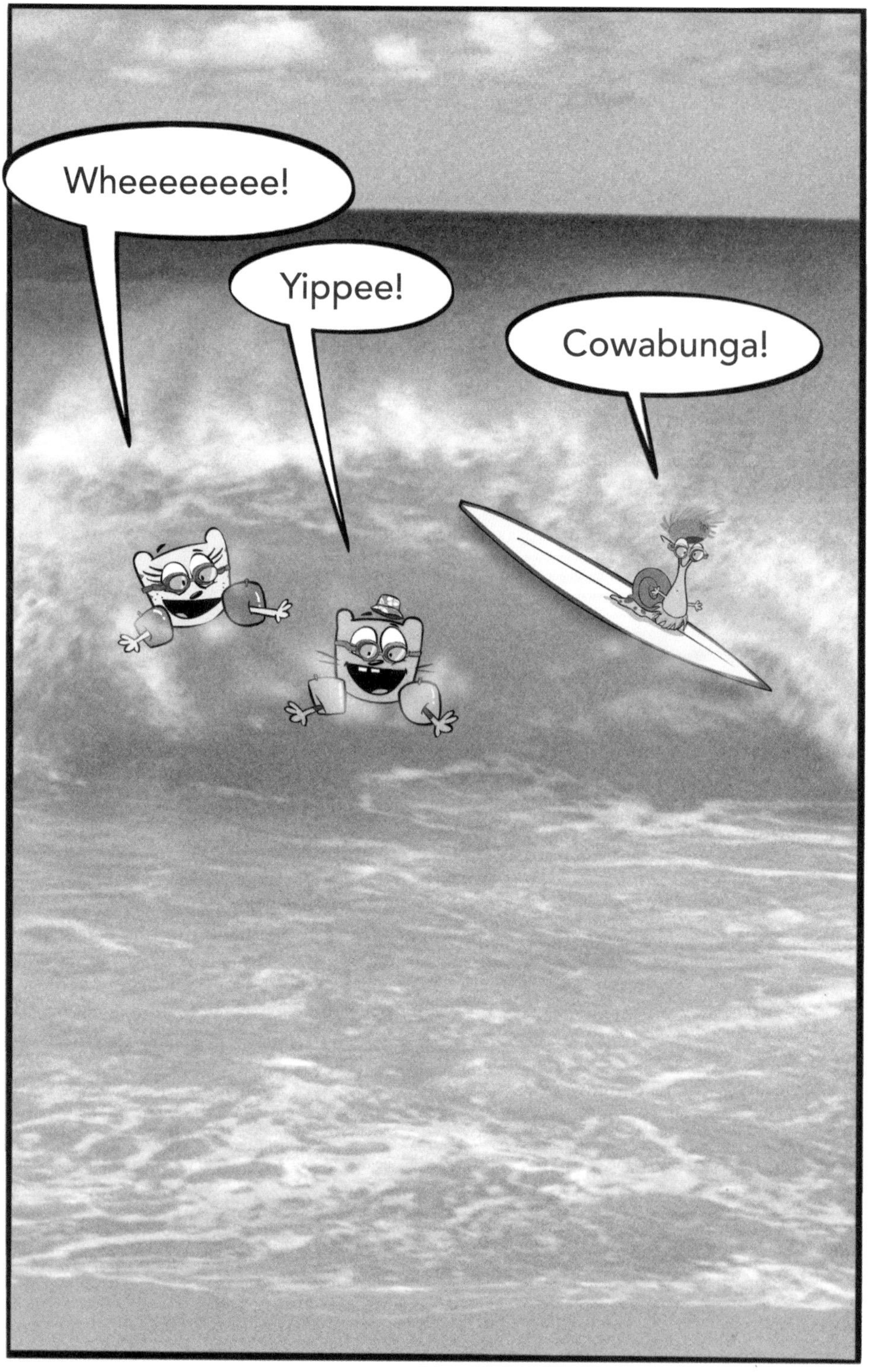
Wheeeeeeee!
Yippee!
Cowabunga!

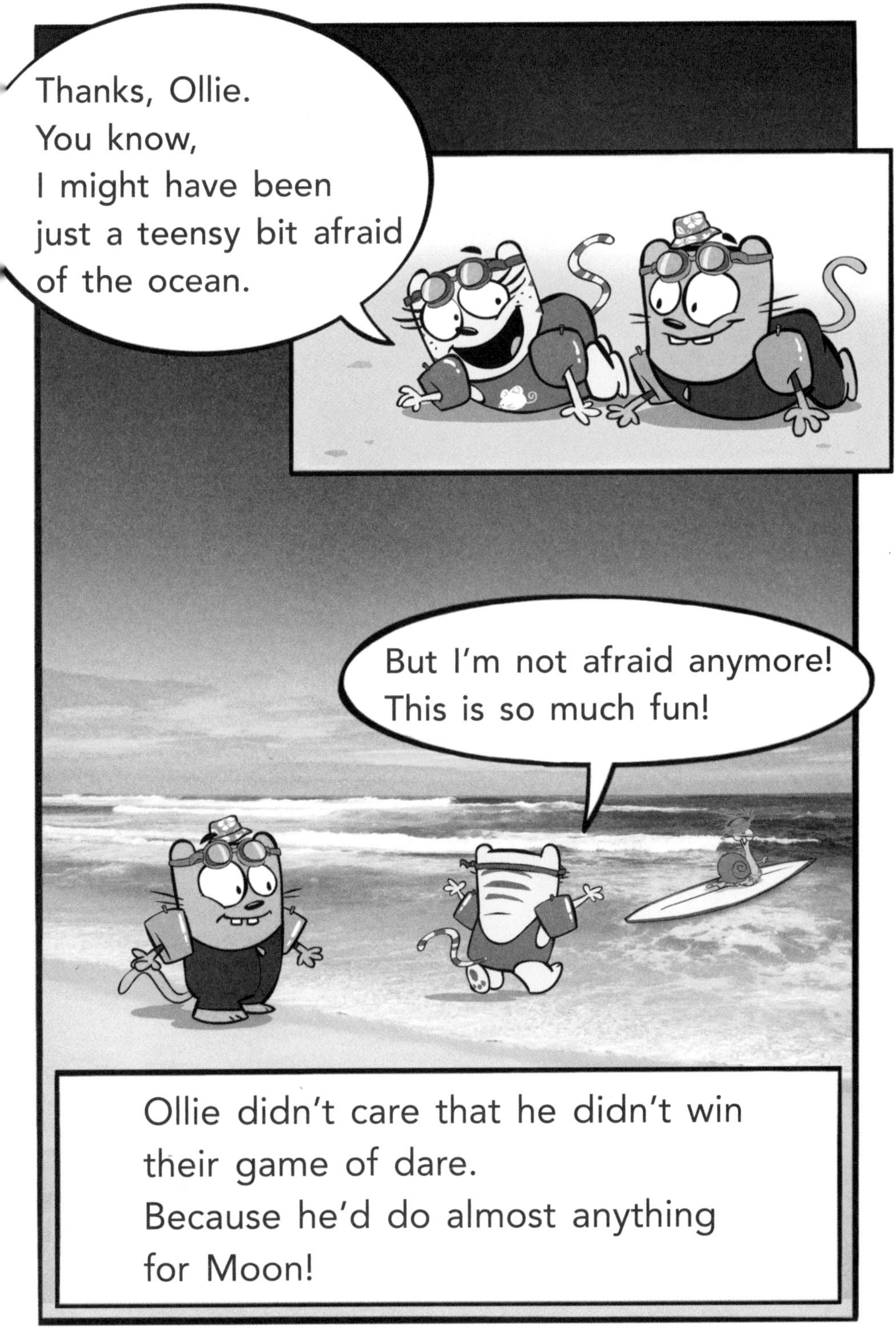
Thanks, Ollie. You know, I might have been just a teensy bit afraid of the ocean.
But I'm not afraid anymore! This is so much fun!
Ollie didn't care that he didn't win their game of dare. Because he'd do almost anything for Moon!

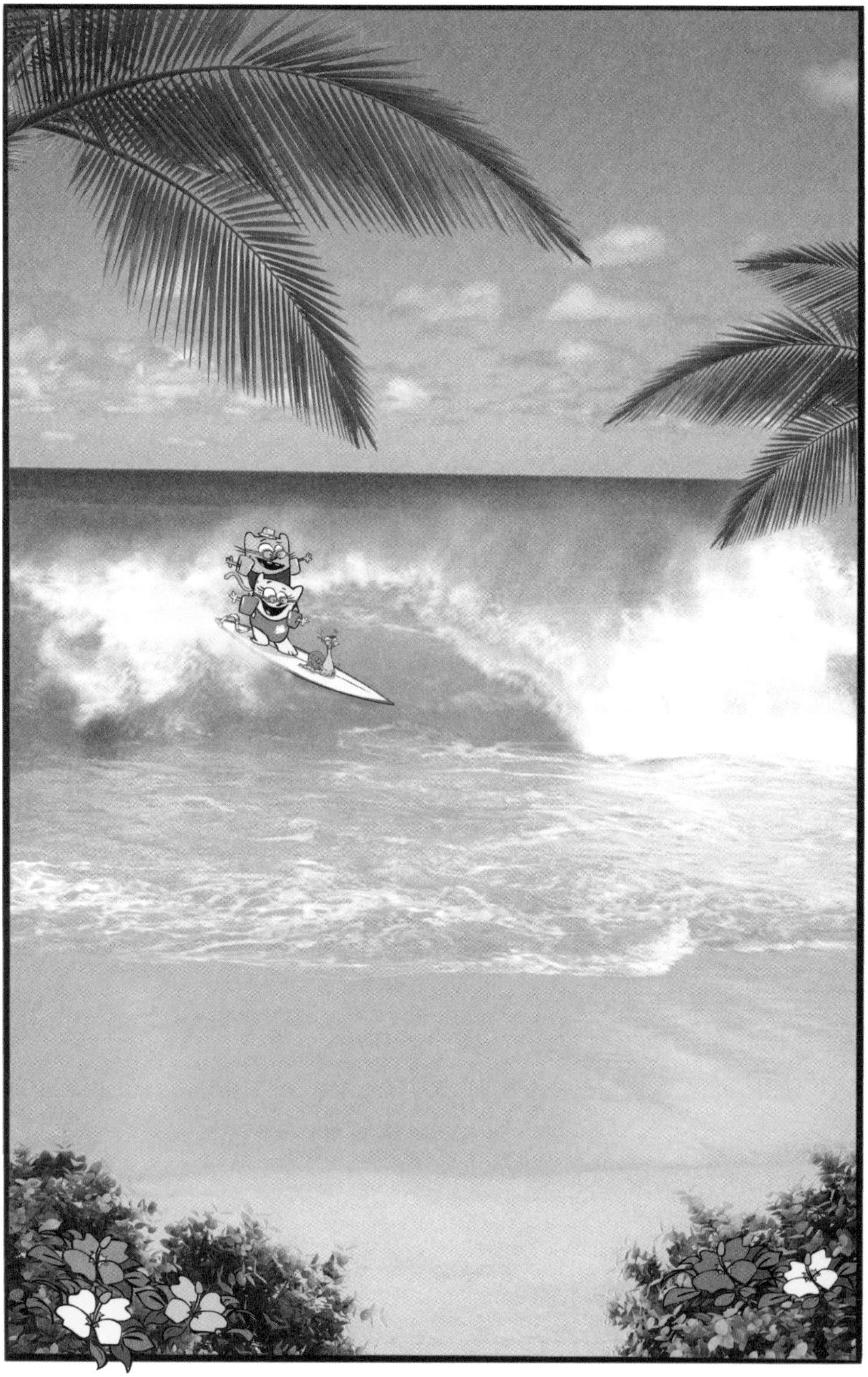